I0729030

Also by R. L. Clayton

Sea Species

The Envoy

Genesis

Visit R. L. Clayton's websites

www.evolutionriver.com

www,rlclaytonbooks.com

ACKNOWLEDGEMENTS

This book could never have been written without the knowledge and experiences of being raised the son of a WASP. WASP, Kids of WASP (KOWS), Friends of WASP (FOWS), Texas Women's University, and others strive to keep alive the spirit and history of WASP while their numbers dwindle away. Their reunions never failed to bring a swelling of pride in me for my mother and the other WASP, and what they accomplished. The changes in our society initiated by them and many others continue today, making us stronger.

My entrance into the community of writers has proven a wonderful experience. The people I've had the privilege to meet and get to know are delightful and brilliant. My special thanks to Melinda Rucker Haynes for her patience and tireless assistance, and thanks to Alexis Powers for her enthusiasm and drive, keeping me going. You both are inspirations to me. How did I get so lucky?

WINGS OF THE WASP

BY R. L. CLAYTON

This book is a work of fiction. Names are the product of the author's imagination. Locations are real, though descriptions imaginary. Any similarities to real people are purely accidental.

Copyright 2015

Prologue

August 1943
Marana Army Air Field

Though it was still morning, Arizona boiled, heat waves like water shimmering across the runway at the Marana Army Airfield. Sgt. Joe Clark watched the two yellow AT-6 trainer aircraft sitting on the runway, their engines idling. He had overhauled the engines on those planes and listened to the loud run-up rumble with pride. With a throaty roar and the release of their brakes, they lumbered down the runway picking up speed, They gracefully left the ground, heading east into the sun toward Avenger Field in Sweetwater, Texas. It was the Women Airforce Service Pilots' (WASP) training field. Clear of the end of the runway, they climbed. Barely above one-hundred feet, one plane's engine stuttered. From midfield, he watched in horror as the big AT-6 tried to turn back over the desert to land.

"No!" screamed Joe. "Belly in. Don't turn!" He ran toward the troubled plane, waving his arms.

The young woman pilot couldn't hear him. Gorge rose in his throat as the plane sank. "Level out! Level out," he screamed.

He saw the plane's bright yellow wingtip clip sagebrush in slow motion. The pilot tried to bring it back to horizontal, but it was too late. Joe closed his eyes and covered his face, willing the inevitable to go away.

From her AT-6, Dawn Dunham saw Mary's plane begin a low, slow turn. Dawn broke left, banked, and came around, yelling over the radio for Mary to belly in.

Mary cried. "I can't I can't. I'm loaded with fuel, and there's no time to dump it. I'll make it back."

Over her headset, Dawn heard the cough of the engine followed by silence. Shock coursed through her as she watched the plane sink. Mary's wingtip hit the ground. The plane cartwheeled across the desert, pieces flying off. Through the dust cloud below, Dawn saw Mary's AT-6 upside-down, wings broken stubs on the fuselage. She turned final approach and lined up to land.

Joe sprinted toward the crash. The cockpit canopy had been torn off. The pilot hung from her harness. He could see she was unmoving. The smell of fuel stung his nose as he neared. The woman stirred, dazed at first. As the first flames licked the nose cowling of the plane, she started struggling with the harnesses. She became frantic in her efforts to free herself as the fire raced along the fuselage.

With a loud whoosh, the fire engulfed her, the searing heat driving Joe back. Tumbling from the cockpit, the pilot rolled on the blazing ground, rose momentarily to her knees, a flaming figure, hand stretched out toward him.

Then her high-pitched screams began, tearing into his soul.

His shrieks and hers rose with the roiling black smoke into the sky, blanking out the sun.

Joe collapsed to the ground, eyes squeezed shut, trying to block out the images. He hugged himself as tears streamed down his face. He'd had dinner with her last night, talked to her. It wasn't supposed to happen this way!

It was supposed to be a minor crash.

PART 1

The War Years, 1943 and Beyond

Chapter 1

To free up men pilots to fight in the European and Pacific theaters, the Women Airforce Service Pilots were trained to take over domestic military flying. The WASP had come in last night to pick up the overhauled planes and deliver them to Texas for the next training class.

The mess hall was unusually quiet when Joe entered. The WASP were eating alone at a corner table. The men were subdued in the women's presence. There were never women in the mess hall. Joe filled his tray with the usual hash and potatoes at the chow line. He glanced at the WASP. The brown-haired one was the taller, with shoulder-length straight hair and an oval face. The other had curly strawberry blonde hair framing a very pretty face.

Their conversation was hushed, but their hand gestures signified airplane talk. Joe was intrigued.

Taking a deep breath, he approached the table. "Mind if I join you?"

They looked up. "If you want," said the brunette, her brown eyes flashing, a smile touching her lips.

Joe took the empty chair. "I'm Joe Clark." He held out his hand.

"Mary Anderson," she said, taking his hand.

"Dawn Dunham," said the blond holding out her hand. Her clear blue eyes held Joe's for a moment. He smelled flowers. Was it perfume or his imagination?

Dawn broke the silence. "What do you do here at the MAAF, Joe?"

Joe looked at his hand clasping hers and quickly released it, stammering, "I'm in maintenance. I'm overhauling the AT-6s you're picking up."

"Are they ready?" asked Mary.

"They will be by morning. I'll probably have to pull an all-nighter, but they'll be ready. I'll run 'em up myself to make sure everything is A-Okay," he said, looking at her.

"You been doing aircraft maintenance long?" asked Dawn.

Joe's eyes returned to her. He forced his lips to work. "The army trained me. Been doing it since I joined in '42." Suddenly self-conscious, he wanted to steer the conversation away from himself. "Did either of you ever fly these particular planes?"

"I trained on the older one," said Dawn. "It always tried to drift to the left on me."

"Yeah, I took care of that," said Joe. "It was a trim control rigging issue. What else have you flown?"

"Dawn's had the most experience. Tell him." Mary looked at her friend.

Dawn turned toward him. "I've flown almost everything. Lately, it's been C-47s mostly, but I did fly a 17, and a 24. My favorite is the P-51 Mustang, though. That plane's swell. It puts me back in my seat, especially with the Rolls Royce engine. As manufacturing ramps up, we'll be taking more of those to shipping ports."

Joe was envious. The Mustang was the hottest plane in the US. What a great job! Flying all over the country in the best planes made. "Where do you fly out of, most of the time?"

Mary smiled. "Romulus, with most deliveries now going to New York ports or Canada."

"Is this your first time in Arizona?" Joe asked, trying to make conversation. He hadn't seen many WASP before.

They both nodded. Mary spoke, "We were supposed to deliver a couple of P-47s to California, but they weren't ready, so they diverted us here to pick these up. It'll give us a chance to see Sweetwater again. It'll be like going home, kinda."

The planes wouldn't be ready until tomorrow. "Where'd they put you for the night?" Joe asked. "There aren't any women's barracks here."

"Yeah, that stopped them for a while after we were dropped off. We're in the hospital." They laughed.

"Those big flight suits don't do much for you gals." Joe blurted out, then reddened, a bit embarrassed.

"The Army doesn't make them in our size. Dawn is simply swimming in hers, even with the cuffs and sleeves rolled up."

"You are a lot smaller than the men."

"It makes those cockpits more roomy, though," said Dawn.

They laughed again. "If you're going back to work, you better eat up before your food gets cold," said Dawn, glancing at his tray.

Joe tore his eyes away and began to gobble his food. Within minutes, he sopped up the last of the gravy with his bread. "Gotta go. See you gals in the morning." He bused his tray, but his mind was on Dawn.

Her eyes followed him out the door.

They were a nice couple of gals, Joe thought as he walked across the dark yard to the hanger. I could get interested in Dawn. She had a twinkle in her eye when she looked at him. Who knows? After tomorrow, he'd probably never see them again.

That's what the war was like.

Chapter 2

Joe's mind was back on task. His footsteps echoed within the huge wooden hanger. Most of the overhaul job was done, so Joe had sent his crew to the barracks for the night. Under the bright lights, he climbed the scaffold and looked into the engine of the AT-6.

Socket wrench in hand, he began checking bolts to see that they torqued to spec. He traced oil lines and fuel lines to see that they were connected correctly and tight. Everything reeked of oil. He wiped his hands and smiled. She was ready. He pulled the safety plugs and closed the cowling. One down and one to go. He checked off the overhaul report form and signed it.

The Marana Army Air Field was where planes came to get new life so they could go back into service in the war effort. The AT-6s were the only planes there tonight. Joe loved working on aircraft.

He had a talent for it. Alone at night, he worked at his own pace, faster than any of his crew. Being crew chief was okay, but he liked to have his hands in the guts of the planes. He hummed to himself as he mounted the scaffolding to the second plane. The sound of the door opening startled him.

"Sergeant, I need to speak with you," announced Captain Allen Rogers.

Joe Clark pulled his head from the engine compartment of the AT-6. With a suppressed groan, he turned on the scaffold and looked down at his Commanding Officer. Captain Allen Rogers was a real hard nose. His uniform was always starched, creases sharp enough to cut butter. He insisted on full protocol – salutes, sir, attention, everything.

What now? He climbed down, came to attention, and saluted. Rogers returned the salute. The Captain was a head taller than Joe with razor cut brown hair and black eyes. His mouth curled into a frown.

"Sergeant, the pilots picking up these planes are Women Airforce Service Pilots. We both know it is only because of the pilot shortage these women are allowed to fly military aircraft. Otherwise, I'd never let them into one of my aircraft. We also know that they aren't as good as men pilots. We need to establish a record of their shortcomings, so I need an incident."

"What do you mean, 'incident,' Captain? What are you talking about?" Joe's mind flashed back to the two women pilots at the mess hall.

"Sergeant, I just want something that will make the pilot look bad. If you leave the service plugs in the engine, it'll choke during takeoff, never get off the ground. She'll roll off the end of the runway and break the undercarriage."

"But they're performing a needed service, sir. They're in this war effort with us."

"Service, Sergeant?" He fixed Joe with a stare, They're not as good as the men. We've got men who are really performing a service. They're away from home and getting shot. Their lives are at risk." The Captain shook his head. "There are things that women aren't made to do."

This didn't sit right. The WASP Joe had seen flew every bit as good as the men. The image of

Dawn smiling at him returned. Creating a wreck felt like cheating "I dunno, Sir. I could get my ass in a sling over this. Someone might get hurt." Joe Clark removed his cap and wiped his forehead, with his greasy hand. He'd been working twelve straight hours. His eyes were burning. He needed rack time. And now this.

The Captain stared at him. His voice hardened. "Joe, we'll pull the plugs before the investigators get here. No one will ever find out. It'll look like she was incompetent and ignored the gauges. If we let these women keep flying, where will it stop. We both know they're not as good as the men pilots. It's for their own protection. We need to get them back in the kitchen. This is the best thing for all of us, them too."

"Are you ordering me to do this, sir?"

"I am but I'm not – know what I mean?"

Joe felt trapped. He couldn't refuse a direct order, but it wasn't right. "Captain Rogers, is this you or did these orders come from command?"

"They came down a long way. This has to be kept on the QT. Tell no one, and I mean NO ONE. Do you understand, Sergeant Clark?"

"Yes, sir." Joe saluted as the Captain spun and left the hanger, the sound of his retreating steps echoing back at Joe.

His shoulders slumped. He could be hung out to dry if something went wrong. Besides, these WASPs had done well. Several had ferried repaired and overhauled planes from here. They flew well. Watching from the ground, he wouldn't know who the pilot was.

Troubled, Joe returned to the scaffold. The checkout went quickly. He checked the blanks beside the items signifying completion of the overhaul. His hand hesitated above the blank for 'Plugs Removed.' He checked it and signed.

Joe cleaned the grease from his hands and went to the shower. The hot water and intense scrubbing did not wash away the dirty feeling of doing something wrong. He finished cleaning up and put on his khakis and headed for the barracks to catch a couple of hours shuteye before reveille.

Sleep didn't come. He tossed and turned in sweat soaked sheets, his knotted stomach threating to reject his dinner.

The MAAF headquarters building was dark and deserted except for the light in Captain Rogers' office. Rogers picked up the phone as soon as it rang.

"Captain Rogers here."

"Major Williams here. Allen, it's Jake. Are we ready for tomorrow?"

"It'll be okay, sir. They're leaving in the morning and I've arranged for a little incident. It won't be big, but with your team, there should be no problem ruling 'Pilot error'. Just make sure it's your team that shows up to investigate."

"Captain, my end's good. I'll have those guys ready to leave first light. They can't cover up everything, so your mechanics have to have their story together."

"I'm using the sergeant in charge, so there will be only him involved. He's with us, so I can take care of him."

"Okay, I'll await your call tomorrow."

Chapter 3

Dawn killed the engine and jumped from her still rolling plane. The column of thick black smoke cast a shadow across the ground as she ran toward the crash, approaching Joe Clark, curled into a ball on the ground. A glance at the inferno seared her eyeballs as the heat singed her skin. Dragging Joe back from the inferno, she asked him, "Joe are you hurt? Joe, can you hear me?"

The fire truck and ambulance raced down the runway. She held Joe, listened to his moans, and looked at the blackened lump that was Mary. The wind shifted, and the smell of smoke and burned flesh caused her to retch. It took all of her self-control to hold down her breakfast. Mind frozen, her heart pounded.

The fire truck passed her. Figures jumped out, pointing hoses at the inferno. Through the ringing in her ears, a voice asked, "Ma'am, are you hurt?"

Dawn looked up. A face swam into focus. "Huh?"

"Are you all right?"

"I'm fine, but I'm not sure about Joe." She looked at the shivering figure she held.

Another man helped her stand. "We'll take care of him. You come with me. We'll check you out."

She stumbled away, looking over her shoulder at the crash, the pyre of her friend.

A corpsman steadied her and helped her into his jeep. Within minutes, he delivered her to the hospital.

The doctor checked her over. "Does anything hurt?" he asked.

"Physically, I'm fine, but my friend…"

"I'm going to give you something. I want you to return to your room and get some rest."

Dawn hardly felt the prick of the needle. She was already numb. An aide helped her stand and took her down the hall to the room she and Mary shared. The drug was slowing her mind, her thoughts sluggish, like walking through mud. The aide helped her into the bed. Before her eyes closed, she looked at Mary's things atop the adjacent bed. Her heart jumped.

Another aide called to the doctor.

"Captain, another patient here."

The doctor entered the examination room looked at the man sitting on the table steadied by the aide. Pulled out the man's dog tags.

"Sergeant Clark, can you hear me?" asked the doctor. There was no response from the slumped figure supported by the two aides. "Sergeant Clark, look at me," ordered the doctor. No response.

He poked Joe with a pin. Joe flinched. "Sergeant Clark, look at me." Slowly, Joe raised his eyes to the doctor. "Watch my finger," he ordered. Joe's eyes moved as he followed the movement of the finger.

"Sergeant Clark, what happened?"

The words "I killed her" rose to Joe's lips, but Captain Rogers' order to not say anything held it inside. Joe pressed his lips together.

"Sergeant Clark, I'm going to keep you here overnight."

Joe nodded. He was awakening as if from a coma. He tried to wave away the syringe the doctor held, but his hand barely moved. The aides wheeled him down the hall.

The doctor wrote up his notes at his desk. He reached for the phone.

"Captain Rogers, this is Captain Weinstein at the hospital. I've sedated both Dawn Dunham and Sergeant Joe Clark. Both are in shock from the crash today."

"Did Clark say anything?"

"No sir, he did not speak. At one point I thought he would, but he remained silent."

"Doctor, I need them to make statements to the investigating team tomorrow."

"Captain Rogers, I cannot promise that.. Dunham is in better shape than Clark, but we'll have to see what they're like tomorrow."

"Thank you, Captain Weinstein. Keep me apprised."

Chapter 4

Lieutenant Mike Albert glanced around Captain Rogers' office. It was stark, steel gray desk, green walls, plain tile floors, nothing personal to be seen. The overhead fluorescent light flickered.

"At ease. Lieutenant Albert, where are you with your investigation?"

"We're finished with the site inspection. Indications are that she ignored the warning lights and tried to take off despite them. Once the engine stalled, she did not belly down on the desert, but tried to bring the plane around and land. It was a classic amateur mistake." He handed Rogers a draft copy of the report.

Rogers placed one hand on it and dialed the hospital. "This is Captain Rogers. Connect me with Captain Weinstein."

"Captain, how are Dunham and Clark doing?"

"Both are much better today. I'm releasing them this afternoon."

Rogers hung up "Lieutenant, you can get your interviews this afternoon. That's all. Dismissed," said Captain Rogers.

The lieutenant saluted and left.

.

Joe Clark approached the blackened ground and hulk of the AT-6. He stood still, holding off his disabling vision of the crash and fire. A crew of men arrived in a truck, unloading shovels. He looked at the blackened pile of ashes that had been Mary Anderson. He choked back a cry. It did not correlate with the young woman he'd spoken with two days ago. The cleanup crew approached the wreck.

"We need to collect the remains and clean this up, sergeant."

"I know. I'll help." He took the shovel from the corporal. Tenderly, Joe used the shovel to place Mary's remains in the body bag. Periodically, he stopped to catch his breath, compose himself. The other members of the crew let Joe handle the remains.

Dawn looked at Lieutenant Albert sitting behind the steel desk. She dreaded this interview. The crash was a raw wound in her brain. She didn't want to revisit it just yet. But she had to.

In the hall, she'd spoken to Joe Clark briefly. His lips hardly moved. She didn't think Joe has said much.

"Miss Dunham, when you saw Mary Anderson's plane slow, what did you do?"

"I contacted her on the radio. She said she was having engine trouble. I heard her engine quit, told her to belly in. She wasn't high enough to bail out."

"What did she do?"

"She told me that with her plane fully fueled and no time to dump it, she didn't consider that an option. She said she was going to bring it around and land."

"You knew that wasn't an option, didn't you?" the lieutenant barked.

"I wasn't in her cockpit!"

"Would you have tried to land?"

"I wasn't in her cockpit."

"That'll be all, Miss Dunham. Dismissed."

Dawn saluted and left the office. Inside, she was fuming. They were trying to pin this on Mary! It wasn't her fault the engine quit.

She exited the headquarters building, looking around at the open desert. She had to be alone. In the distance was a spike of a peak – Pichaco Peak, the map said. It was too far for a destination, but it was a direction. Dawn grabbed her canteen from the hospital.

Away from the airfield, the desert heat soaked into her and baked the anger out. Her walk was a mindless trek until she noticed the sun low on the western horizon, casting a golden glow over everything. Clouds had built up over the distant Catalina mountains to the east,. The bottoms were black, streaks of lightning reaching for the ground. The cloud tops, easily above 50,000 feet, were so bright, their glare hurt her eyes. A storm was coming. Dawn turned back toward the base. Though she didn't want to be around people, she didn't want to get caught in the maelstrom.

Chapter 5

The hanger was silent, only Joe and the surviving AT-6 occupying the cavernous space. The scene he couldn't erase played in his mind. When the screams started, his own cries echoed back at him. He had to talk to someone – Captain Rogers.

Was it late? He didn't know as he dialed. When the phone rang on the other end, doubts surfaced, and Joe started to hang up.

"Captain Rogers here. Who the hell is this?"

"Captain Rogers, i... it's Sergeant Clark. Sir, I have to see you!" Joe panted in a panicked voice.

"Calm down, Sergeant. I'll meet you in the repair hanger in fifteen minutes."

Why had he done it? Leaving the plugs in the engine seemed like such a small thing. He had been sure the plane couldn't take off. How had the pilot even been able to get enough power to get it off the runway? Once in the air, why did she try to turn around? She could have dumped fuel and just bellied in. There was plenty of desert. But she hadn't, and her screams wouldn't get out of his head.

The investigating team left today, assuring everybody that the cause was *'Pilot Error,'* but Joe knew differently. The hanger door opened and Captain Rogers entered. Even with this short notice, his uniform was crisp, his face had a freshly scrubbed look. Joe opened his mouth to speak, but nothing came out. He came to attention and saluted. The captain returned it.

"At ease, Sergeant." Rogers looked at his crew chief. He was a mess – shirt tail hanging out, shirt mis-buttoned, boots unlaced, eyes red. "Are you having a problem?" Rogers asked gruffly. He watched Joe's eyes lower to his boots. His voice was weak as he answered.

"Yes sir. I haven't been able to sleep since it happened. This is bad, sir. I keep hearing her screams, and when I close my eyes, I see her burning body fall out of the cockpit."

Rogers had to snap Joe out of this funk. He was losing it, his confession could be a threat.

"Joe, it was her fault. If she'd been a better pilot, she would have just set it down. What a fool for trying to bring it around with no power. Any decent pilot knows that. It's the problem with these women. Sure, we need them now so our boys can go overseas and fight, but that won't last forever. When our good men return, they'll need those pilot jobs to support their families. These women don't have families or even husbands. We need them now, but we have to show that the men deserve those jobs. It's as simple as that.

"Sergeant, your reaction to this woman's death is exactly the reason we cannot let women into this world. Women can't handle the job. Men cannot handle their deaths."

Joe looked at the AT-6. "Sir, we murdered that pilot," he exclaimed with a shudder. "She was only doing her job and helping in the war effort. We killed her for that. Dawn, the other pilot, she's passing a hat around to get enough money to send the body home. The Army won't even send the body back to her family. What kind of treatment is that?"

With tears blurring his eyes, Joe turned back to the Captain. "It's not right, sir. We're going to hell for this."

Rogers stiffened, then softened his posture. "Sergeant… Joe, listen. I know this turned out badly. Especially for you since it was you who left the plugs in and helped move the body out of the wreckage."

"Bad! I had to use a shovel, and I still didn't get all of her. The only thing that was in one piece was her wings!" Joe screamed in a ragged voice.

The captain reached under his jacket and pulled out a flask. "Here, you need this." He handed it to Joe.

Joe took a large gulp, then coughed as the raw whiskey burned his throat, twisting his stomach. He wiped his mouth with the back of his sleeve. "Sir, I can't keep this in. Every time I walk in this hanger, I see that plane sitting there ready to kill her. When I look at the runway, I see that burning wreck. I'm going to my priest tomorrow. This is tearing me up inside. Her shrieks just won't stop."

"Joe, take the flask with you. Come see me first thing in the morning. I'll get you help." Captain Rogers clapped him on the back. "In the meantime, don't talk to anybody, not even your priest. I'll help you get through this. Remember, Joe, you left the plugs in, but this was really her fault. She just was a woman, not a real pilot." He turned and walked out of the hanger.

Joe watched the door for a long time. What could the captain do? There were no do-overs here. They had sabotaged that plane and killed the pilot. It didn't matter that some hotshot combat pilot would eventually get a job out of this. Joe had destroyed his own soul.

Chapter 6

Captain Rogers went to his office rather than back to his quarters. He closed the door and sat as his desk. With a deep sigh, he rang the base operator and had him put a call through to Colonel Arnold.

"Bob, Allen Rogers here. Sorry to disturb you at this hour, but I'm having a problem after that crash two days ago. Yeah, it's a shame that the pilot got killed. It wasn't supposed to happen, but we knew it was a possibility when we started this program. That's not making it any easier on my maintenance sergeant, Joe Clark. He's really torn up. I don't think he'll hold up."

Rogers listened a moment and spoke, "Yes sir, the inquiry ended this afternoon. They ruled '*Pilot Error*,' of course. The other pilot, Dawn Dunham, is going to accompany the body back to the family tomorrow. Through the whole investigation, she looked over the shoulders of the inspectors. I don't think she liked the ruling.

"No, I don't think she saw the engine plugs. The inspectors got the evidence of those out as soon as the wreckage cooled. Anyway, she'll be gone tomorrow. It's my maintenance sergeant I'm worried about," said Rogers. "He's not holding up well. If he breaks, his story cold hurt us."

Allen listened to the major and agreed. "Yes sir, I can do that. I hate to lose him as a mechanic, sir. He's the best I have. Okay, if he doesn't come out of this, I'll cut orders for him to go to Fort Glenn on Umnak Island, Alaska. It'll sure be a change. It's been over a hundred degrees here the last week. That'll keep his mind off this mess, give him a chance to recover. Okay, Thanks Bob."

As Allen put the phone down, he heard a click. His eyes flew open. Had someone been listening? He flung the door open and ran into the hall. All the offices were dark, the Staff Sergeant's desk empty. He hurried back to his desk and dialed the company operator. "Corporal, is anybody there with you?"

"No sir. Do you need me to place another call?"

"Son, you realize that this call was confidential."

"Absolutely, sir. All I know is the number you had me call."

"Corporal, I want you to delete that call from the log. Is that understood?"

"Yes, sir."

Rogers strode down the hall, looking into each darkened office. He didn't know if the corporal lied or if there had been someone else, but he had better get to the bottom of it. He sat behind his desk nervously flipping a pencil. Could there have been an eavesdropper? Was it his imagination?

The faint click of a door being eased shut went unheard.

Dawn Dunham glanced behind as she scurried from shadow to shadow back to the hospital. She was shaken. Something was wrong, and it wasn't limited to this base. Entering her room unnoticed, she crawled into her bunk, fully dressed. In the dark, her mind roiled.

The investigation team had hammered questions at her, forcing her to put into words the images seared into her brain. It was a pain beyond anything she'd ever experienced. "Why did Mary try to come back around to land? Didn't she know the engine failure procedures? Did she accidently hit the kill switch? Did she try to restart the engine? Why didn't she just belly in?"

Over and over Dawn was forced to describe the death of her friend. The vision of that figure tearing at her burning clothes then falling onto the fuel soaked ground and being engulfed consumed her mind. After her walk, she sought the solitude of her room at the hospital. The air within was still, the bed next to hers empty. The spirit of her friend gone.

She'd been ordered to stay and assist with the investigation, but now she had to get out. Dawn had shunned company, eating from the snack bar. Unable to stay in her room except to sleep, and there wasn't much of that. Everywhere she looked, it reminded her of Mary. She sought solitude in dark and empty offices. She had picked up the phone to call Mary's mom when that call from Captain Rogers came on the line. It was an accident. She wasn't trying to eavesdrop.

The chills of that call froze her. Was this intentional? Who was responsible? How high did this go? And more importantly, who would she tell? Her first order of business was to get out of here without anybody suspecting what she had overheard. Dawn shivered and pulled the blanket under her chin. The images of her friend's death were now overlaid by a dark cloud of suspicion.

Chapter 7

Joe stood at attention, his eyes glued to the office wall behind Captain Allen Rogers. His head hurt, he swayed, the half-empty hip flask in his pocket calling to him.

"Sergeant Clark, what's going on with you? It's been a week since the crash. I've had reports of you showing up drunk. You reek of alcohol, and it's ten-o'clock in the morning! An inspector found an oil line not connected on a plane you certified. Explain yourself."

Joe's eyes shifted to the Captain. "Sir, I just can't get the crash out of my head. That woman's screams burn into me every time I close my eyes. I can't eat or sleep."

Captain Rogers eyed the sad mess before him. Joe's face was gaunt and drawn – his eyes sunk back and red-rimmed. His coveralls looked two sizes too large. "Sergeant Clark... Joe, I'm going to get you away from this base. A change of scenery will pull you out of this. You were my best mechanic, and you can be again. But you've got to get over this. An accident happened, and that's what it was – an accident. None of us ever intended to have that girl die in the crash. She died because she didn't follow procedure. She was a bad pilot and shouldn't have been in the cockpit. You and I both know what happens to bad pilots eventually. It wasn't your fault, it was hers."

Rogers watched his words bounce off Joe's head. None of it sunk in. Guilt would not let him blame anybody but himself, and it was eating him up. Even to Rogers, his own words sounded like he was trying to convince himself rather than Joe. At the word, "dismissed," a tearful Joe saluted and left the office.

Rogers watched the slumping back of his top mechanic stumbling out the door. A good mechanic, but not tough enough for this man's army, and a definite liability to those around him and himself.

He yelled for his clerk. "Cut orders for Sergeant Clark transferring him to Fort Glenn Army Air Base effective tomorrow. I need him up there."

Maybe the weather and the isolation of a base seventy miles west of the Umnak Island Naval Base would snap him out of his funk. The major push by the Japanese to take the Aleutians had been turned back. The battle for Attu Island had been the costliest of the war.

Known for some of the worst weather in the world, the forces battled each other and the elements. It would give Clark something else to think about. The invasion of Kiska Island marked the end of Japanese efforts and forces were being moved elsewhere. The Aleutians still had importance as a northern route to Japan, so forces would remain. Clark was unlikely to get into trouble there.

Captain Rogers shook his head. It was for the good of women everywhere that they not be exposed to the rigors of a man's world. If this were allowed here where would it stop? America would never stand for women in combat.

Chapter 8

Joe peered out the barracks window at fog so thick it was a grey wall. What a miserable place Ft. Glenn was. In the three months he'd been here, he had yet to see the sun. The cold seeped through your clothes into you, down to the bone. Joe looked around the rec room. Guys were playing pool and listening to the radio. They talked to each other trying to convince themselves it wasn't as bad as it really was.

Weather like this grounded all planes – again. They overhauled newly overhauled engines just for something to do. In the corner of the room sat a small Christmas tree. Trees were in short supply up here, the island mostly semi-frozen mush. The decorations were whatever the crews could come up with. There were baubles from home and polished rejected aircraft parts. It was a desperate attempt at Christmas spirit.

Christmas Eve. Gosh, it didn't seem like it. One day just blended into another here. Today looked like yesterday – wet and cold. Some of the guys got presents of stale cookies and wooly scarves. Joe envied them, not because of the gifts. but because they had someone who cared. Sometimes he just wanted to walk out and keep going. But too many guys depended on him to keep them in the air.

This place was a dumping ground. None of these guys seemed like the "on the ball" type. Joe's final inspections always turned up problems – some of which would get a pilot killed. He really couldn't live with that.

For Christmas, the CO brought in extra beer for the enlisted and special eggnog for the officers.

"Joe, you want my ration of eggnog?" asked Captain Smith. "I don't drink."

"Sure, sir. Thanks. Merry Christmas." Captain Smith was a nice enough looking guy, too tall for a pilot, though. He had kind brown eyes, and smiled a lot, so he probably washed out of any sort of combat position. He was a bit of a prig, a real "by-the-book" type, but not as bad as Rogers. None of the other officers liked him, but he was good to his crews. He was always getting things from his wife. He showed Joe a picture of his family once. They were on a farm in Utah. Pretty wife and 5 kids. It was a nice picture.

The nightmares came less often, not because Joe was getting over them, but because their work at just staying warm was so draining. The nights seemed endless, the days brief flashes of grey. This world was so foreign, it was easy to leave everything behind in that 'other world', the one of reality. Joe closed the door on that world.

Booze was hard to come by, so Joe went cold turkey and threw himself into work. Planes leaving his crew were better than new. The pilots appreciated that.

The weather really turned bad the day after Christmas. The temperature was at freezing, so the wet fog stuck and made an ice coating. Luckily, planes were not flying much. They couldn't be de-iced fast enough. Some of the guys made New Years Resolutions. Joe mused, what did he want to change in 1945? He wanted to get out of here, but that was not going to happen. Besides, that wasn't a resolution. One bleak day marched on the heels of the last.

The Ides of March! Last night a "willowaw" (a violent squall) struck and wrecked a number of supply boats. Joe was a mess too. A plane came in through the fog, overshooting the runway and crashing. Jesus! It all came back. His guys had to carry him away from the wreckage. He woke up in sickbay, remembering nothing. They gave him stuff so he could sleep. After a couple of days, he was out and back to work. A question haunted Joe, one of those you can't define, but it was there. Every time he tried to define it, is skittered away.

Sundays were his days off. Since his bout in the hospital, the guys acted differently around him. They'd stop talking whenever he came near. Some of the things he ranted about were too weird. He was different around the planes, too – always sure there was something he missed or forgot. He kept going back. Joe knew something would happen because the planes were piling up, not released back into service.

His CO, Captain Smith had to talk to him. "Joe, you've got to quit obsessing. You're not signing off on planes that are perfect. We have to release them back to the pilots. These planes have to get back in the air."

"Sir, when I look at a plane, all I see are things going wrong. I have to keep checking. I can't be responsible for a pilot's death."

"Joe, we can only do our best. We have to move on."

Joe sighed. That was easy enough for him to say. Joe had to talk to Father Morrison. He had to let some of this out. He couldn't say anything about the crash in Arizona. He was not ready to do that yet. Maybe someday.

"It's Friday the thirteenth, sir," said Joe.

Captain Smith laughed. "It's just a superstition, Joe."

"I know, sir, but I said prayers with my fingers crossed. I'm going to do everything to make sure things go well."

"Joe, do your job. We're flying a lot of patrols because it's spring." The captain laughed. "It's not much different from winter. The rumors are that the war in Europe is winding down. You probably noticed people are being sent to England."

Lucky bastards! Joe thought. The captain didn't use many curse words, so he restrained himself around Captain Smith.

The announcement of VE Day roused them at reveille! Everybody went crazy. It was hard to dance in a parka, but they did it. Captain Smith wore an ear-to-ear grin. He clapped Joe on the back.

"Joe, Japan has to realize the end is coming. Tokyo Rose said they were going to fight to the last woman and child. I expect a buildup here in preparation for that invasion. We need to be ready to handle that."

The expected troop buildup for the invasion of Japan didn't happen, though the air sorties increased. B-29s came in, but they flew out and didn't return. The invasion was going to be by a southern route. This was a pretty miserable place to muster troops in invasion numbers. Joe and his crew saw more aircraft as the war emphasis shifted to the Pacific. Activity was ramping up. It kept them busy. Tension was in the air.

"What's going on, sir?" Joe asked Captain Smith.

"Something's in the works, but I don't know what. It's been very hush hush."

Captain Smith had the crews gather around him. He stood on a bench so they all could hear him. "Gentlemen, yesterday a new type of super bomb was dropped on Japan. It was the biggest bomb ever made and wiped out most of Hiroshima. It's an effort to convince Japan to surrender unconditionally. Nobody wants to invade Japan."

A super bomb. Joe didn't know what to think about that, except a light at the end of this war tunnel now appeared.

Two days later Captain Smith called everybody together in the main hanger. He stood on a workbench to make an announcement to his crews.

"Gentlemen, another super bomb was dropped yesterday. It's called an 'Atomic Bomb' whatever that is. What this means is this war is going to end, without thousands more dead American soldiers."

The roar drowned out anything else. Again, everyone danced. Whiskey appeared.

"We're going home, sir," Joe said to Captain Smith, holding a cup of whiskey.

"We are. Joe, I believe I'll try a sip of that."

The captain's eyes watered, he coughed for 5 minutes. Everybody laughed.

It rained for four days, but nobody cared. Troop ships were coming! Orders came down to pack things, and the planes headed for Cold Harbor. They were going home!

Chapter 9

It was a miracle day. The fog was gone, but it was not sunny. From the breakroom window, Joe watched the troop transport approach. At last, he was getting out of this God forsaken place. Christ! He had been in Alaska for two years and was never warm. He never wanted to see snow or ice again, even in his scotch. A thousand pairs of eyes followed the ship as it crawled toward them. One would think that just the force of so many guys wanting it to be here would move it faster. He went outside, standing on the ramp overlooking the dock. He wasn't alone.

"Looking forward to going home, sir?" Joe asked Captain Smith.

"Last year after we kicked the Japs out of Kiska and the north Pacific, I hoped to get to go stateside. I understood we had to stay. Now with the end of the war, I'm looking forward to being a farmer again, having Jane and the kids around. How about you, Joe? Looking forward to going home?"

"Well, at least back to the States, sir. I'm not sure where home is now. I hardly remember Mom and Dad, being so young when they died in a car accident."

"I'm sorry, Joe. I didn't know that you lost your parents."

"Mom's sister, Aunt Ellie became my mom. With no husband and four kids, I became another mouth to feed, but I had nowhere else to go. Lucky I had a knack for things mechanical because I sure didn't do well in school. My job as a helper at the repair shop brought in a few bucks, and Lord knows we needed it. Clothes were passed down until they were mere threads with patches on patches. We were vegetarians, but not by choice." Joe sighed at the memory.

"That's not home?" asked Captain Smith.

Joe looked out the window. The transport ship was no closer than the last time he looked. The 'watched pot' syndrome, he supposed. He looked back at the captain.

"I haven't thought of Aunt Ellie for a while. Lying about my age to enlist at sixteen didn't make her unhappy to see me go. We did hug, and she wished me well. I wrote her once, but I never heard back. She can't write and probably never has the time." Joe's eyes moistened. "I keep sending her most of my pay, 'cause she and the kids need it more than me. At least the Army feeds me and gives me a bed."

Joe looked back at the approaching transport ship. "Sir, the Army Air Corp has been my home, and they're going to kick me out. Not that I'm blue about that, it's just where do I go now?"

The captain remained silent for a moment. "Joe, if you need a place to stay until you get your feet on the ground, you can try your hand at farming. We could use another pair of hands, a mechanic too."

"Thank you, sir. I'll surely think about that." He turned to watch the almost stationary ship. The captain wandered away to talk with others of his men.

The last letter Joe got from Dawn was a month ago. He wrote her ten letters to every one she wrote back. She had family, so her writing time had to be shared with them. He understood that.

At the end of last year, they shut down the WASP program and told the women to go home. Dawn did for a while. He got a few more letters from her then. But she'd seen and done too much to stay in a small town, so she went to California with a bay-mate of hers from the WASP. Her last letter said she was working as a mechanic on some new secret program.

Imagine her, a mechanic! They had something in common now beside the tragedy in Marana. He would like to know more about what she did, but she couldn't write about it. She did invite him to come visit her when he got out, so Pasadena was his first destination. Okay, He was nervous about seeing her. Somehow, the inert ship had made the harbor. It was time to board. He grabbed his meager duffle from the barracks and got in line.

Being packed in like sardines didn't bother anybody. They were going home. GIs laughed, slapped each other on the back, and told stories of girlfriends. Joe chose the solitude of the deck and the chill. He was by himself at the rail when Captain Smith walked over.

"Thought about my offer, Joe?"

"Captain Smith, that's the most generous thing I've received in a long time. There's a girl I've been writing. I'd like to see her. Guess I'll just knock around California for a while."

"I understand. Joe, you're a good mechanic. My offer is always open. You'll find something." He clapped Joe on the back, smiled, and moved away.

From the bow of the ship, Joe pictured himself moving through not only space but time, toward… he didn't know what. At last the cold forced him inside.

Chapter 10

Port Seattle! Guys crowded the rail to be the first off, but they'd all get there so why rush. Part of Joe wanted to get ashore, but another part hesitated to leave. A new life awaited. Nobody's waiting for me, he thought. Yeah, he'd let the guys with wives and girlfriends waiting go first. There was a crowd under the lights on the dock waving like crazy.

With September just around the corner, it was warm. At least the rain had stopped. Wow! He'd never seen so many deuce-and-a-halfs lined up. That was their transport to the bus and train stations. Trucks for the enlisted, busses for the officers. The Army never changed.

It took three hours to disembark from the ship, get on the trucks, and get to the train station. Joe's train didn't leave until morning, so he slept on the floor along with about five hundred other guys. It was hard to walk across the floor to the head, and that place stunk. Captain Smith was putting together some guys to clean it. Joe faded into the back, didn't want that duty.

"Joe, don't forget my offer. I'd like to have you working with me on the farm." He held out his hand.

Joe shook it. "Sir, it was a pleasure serving under you. I have your address if I change my mind."

"Good luck, Joe. I hope things work out with your girl." He waved as he boarded his train to Salt Lake City.

Joe's train was crowded, but at least he got a seat. The aisles were full. He switched off, giving others a chance to sit every hour or two. Most of the guys were excited, talking and laughing. Joe kept to himself.

Anxiety about this trip filled him. Part of him was excited about being back. Another part was bubbly about seeing Dawn again, but he was edgy too. Doubts crept in. The visions of that awful crash in Marana had faded, but the pain remained. What did she feel? He wondered. The jostling of the train and all the bodies around him went unnoticed.

The trip from Seattle took a day. He had to sleep standing up for part of it. From the train depot, he caught a bus into Pasadena. His bus heading east wasn't leaving for a few hours, so he went outside to wait. Sunshine and warm temperatures made him close his eyes in pure joy. He basked on a bench like a lizard on a rock.

"Hey, Clark. You want to go to the beach with us?" Three of his crewmates called from a taxi.

"Nah, I've seen enough ocean for a while."

"Yeah, but it's warm in California."

"You guys go ahead. I feel like a nap." They laughed as the taxi pulled away.

He dozed off, nearly missing the last call. Hurrying onto the bus, he found it wasn't crowded. There obviously were not many people heading east on this route. Dawn hadn't told him much about Muroc except it was dry and hot.

The buildings of Pasadena gave way to orchards. The bus began climbing mountains, taking forever up this road. He couldn't remember ever taking so many switchbacks.

At the top, the bus stopped to let the engine cool. Joe walked around a little. From the viewpoint, he looked out into the valley of the desert beyond.

"Quite a view, isn't it," said the driver. "I never get tired of it." He walked back to the bus.

The vista went on forever. At the driver's call, they re-boarded, and the bus started to wind down the mountain.

He got off at the bus stop in Bakersfield to stretch his legs and get some air. Dry and hot only described it like cold and wet described Umnak Island. As soon as he stepped off the bus, a blast of wind struck, sucking every drop of moisture out of his skin. It was September, so he could only imagine what the 'hot' described.

The desert was so flat. In the distance were blue mountains.

"How far away are those mountains?" he asked the driver.

"About a hundred miles."

"Wow! The look so close, just the other side of that lake."

The driver laughed. "That's a mirage" he said. "It's just heat waves."

The desert seemed so clean and clear compared to Alaska. After the rest stop, they continued through flat featureless land, arriving at the town of Mojave., It was where the public transportation ran out. There were only ten buildings.

Chapter 11

Joe was the last passenger on the bus, and the only one getting off in Mojave. It was a town in name only. It had a gas station, a diner with attached broken down motel, a general store with a post office, and a few houses scattered across the landscape. No trees anywhere.

The temperature was pleasant, but dust stung his face as he entered the gas station/bus stop. Joe stepped around the register to the telephone booth. Dawn's clear voice was music.

"Joe! You made it. I'll be off work in a couple of hours. Go to the diner, and I'll see you there."

"Which diner?" he asked.

She laughed. "See you at Melba's in a couple of hours."

He'd never been in a place where he could see so much of emptiness at one time. Leaving his dufflet at the diner, he took a walk to stretch his legs again. Three laps around the town, and he returned to Melba's for water. He felt like a piece of jerky.

In Alaska, he wasn't able to do a lot of walking because of the weather – rain, sleet, snow, wet fog. The land here really was filled with nothing, there were hardly any bushes, and those were only inches high. It was flat alkali with purple mountains in the distance floating above the shimmering mirage of water. What a change, from cold and wet with greenery everywhere to white, dry, and dusty. There was wind, though, and in the late afternoon, it was strong.

Mojave didn't need sidewalks – the ground being hard packed. He was one of two people at the counter. The other guy wore the largest straw hat Joe'd ever seen. The aroma of fried chicken reminded him he hadn't eaten since breakfast. He wanted to wait to have dinner with Dawn, so when the waitress asked, he ordered apple pie. It had been a while since he'd eaten anything other than GI food. That pie made him realize for the first time that he really was out of the military. The pie wasn't good, it was great! Just as he finished his third cup of coffee, the door opened. Dawn stood in the doorway looking at him.

"Hey, Joe. Whatta ya know?"

Coming from her, he liked it. From everyone else it grated on him. They hadn't seen each other in two years, and those weren't kind years to him. Joe became conscious that his shirt and pants were creased and wrinkled from wearing them two days straight. He had three days growth on his face, and he probably smelled.

Instead of the baggy flight suit he had last seen Dawn in, she wore in a flared skirt and white blouse. Her hair was shoulder length and as blond as he remembered. They approached each other, unsure of what was next. He took her hand to shake it, but she threw her arms around him. The aroma of fresh flowers filled his head. She felt like heaven. They both had so much to say that nothing came out. He led her to a table.

"Dinner?" he asked, not able to say anything more.

"The fried chicken is really good," they both said at the same time. Their laughter was like the sunlight that only occasionally penetrated the fog in Ft. Glenn. It woke him up to the fact that there was a wonderful world out there. The conversation that followed etched into his memory like an old record.

Wiping her fingers, Dawn said, "They're looking for mechanics at Muroc. You want to talk to them?"

"You mean move here?"

"Maybe you better see it first. Muroc might be worse than Alaska."

"Naw, You got sunshine here. What do I need to do?"

"Let me talk to my CO and get you an interview. Meantime, you'll have to stay here. There's no motel in Muroc, only base housing."

"Yeah, I can do that. Anything else I need to know?"

"Work starts early, so I need to go, but I'll call you at the motel tomorrow."

His mind began to wrap around what he'd agreed to. Before he could move, she rose and kissed him on the cheek.

"See ya tomorrow."

And she was out the door. The room seemed empty when she left, but his cheek tingled. Questions flooded in.

Chapter 12

He liked the Mojave Oasis Motel lobby. It had a western flavor with a wood floor and several wooden benches. They, like the paneling and the desk, were made of pine. Indian blankets and pottery decorated the walls. It was neat and clean. The grizzled man behind the desk was reading a two-day old newspaper. He looked up as Joe approached.

"Got a room?" he asked.

"Got lots of rooms. You want one with a view?"

"View of what?"

The old man cackled. "You want to see the sun coming up or the sun going down?"

He picked one facing east because he had always been an early riser. It was a no frills room; a single bare bulb hanging from the ceiling, furniture of the same heavy yellow pine as the motel lobby, paneling of rough sawn pine, a washstand with ewer and a mirror on the wall above it. A towel hung from a hook. The bathroom was down the hall. His room was stuffy and warm, and when he pushed the thin curtains aside to open the window, he looked out into darkness. Joe needed a last stroll before bed.

The night was moonless, but the Milky Way was brilliant, cutting a swath of light across the sky. It's been so long since he'd been able to see so many stars, and it took his breath away. Joe took it to be a sign of good things to come. The wind had calmed, but the temperature was falling and gave him a shiver. The blackness of the sky sucked the heat away.

Sparse pinpricks of light from a few buildings dotted the landscape. He was amazed that once his eyes adjusted, he had no problem picking his way along the desert flats solely by starlight. Was this where he wanted to be? He liked the clean feel of the desert air. Without humidity, it didn't press down on him. He liked being able to see for a hundred miles. He could get used to a land without trees.

What kind of work were they doing at Muroc? She couldn't tell him, but he'd see what it was like when he went for the interview. If Mojave was any indication, he might start to miss trees before long.

The question that pushed everything else aside was what about Dawn? They'd only written letters. Well he did most of the writing. She was a swell kid. He could easily fall for her. The last thing he needed was a disaster, and it brought him up short thinking about it.

They had to discuss the crash that had killed her friend. That had to happen before they could develop a relationship, and he knew he wanted a relationship with her. It was going to be a shock to her because she didn't know anything.

After he confessed his complicity in Mary's murder, would she hate him. Would she still want him? The thought of telling her scared him to death, but it had to be done. He couldn't begin a relationship on a lie, even one of omission. It was a huge worry. He had to tell her the next day.

Sleep wouldn't come – wondering about Muroc, worrying about Dawn, and the nightmare of the crash that haunted his mind. He still felt her kiss. This had become bigger than he thought it would, and so fast!

In Alaska, he worked to exhaustion every night and slept in a dreamless state. That crash on the fog-shrouded runway in Umnak brought the nightmares back and put him on sick call for a week. Now the horror of Mary's crash and the terror of Dawn despising him roiled his mind. How was he to tell her? He couldn't just blurt out, "I killed your friend!"

He had to tell her, and he had to do it tomorrow. Putting it off would weaken his resolve. One more scotch and maybe he'd get some sleep.

Chapter 13

Joe read every magazine and brochure in the motel. He walked until Mojave was a barely discernible speck on the horizon behind him. He bought a book at the general store and read half of that. With Dawn working, he had nothing to do, except worry. The knock on his door was a welcome diversion.

"Mr. Clark, there's a phone call for you."

Joe jumped up. "I'll be right there."

When he reached the front desk, he grabbed the receiver.

"Hey, Joe. Whatta ya know?" Dawn's voice sparkled in his ear.

"Dawn, are you coming to town soon? I've exhausted the entertainment possibilities."

"Ha ha. I bet you have. Yeah, I'll be there in an hour. Can you hang on that long?"

"That will be six more laps around town, but I can make it."

Her laughter lifted him, pushing the onerous task ahead into the background.

Back in his room, he rehearsed what he was going to say. He wrote an outline and rehearsed some more. The knock on the door startled him.

"Hey, Joe. Let's get some dinner. I'm starved."

"Yeah, me too."

They were the only customers in the diner. Joe guided Dawn to a booth near the back.

Dawn smiled up at the waitress. "Hey, Meg. How's business?"

"Better now that you're here."

"What's the special today?" Dawn asked.

"It's Thursday, so chicken fried steak, mashed potatoes with gravy, green beans, and roll is the blue plate special. Apple pie is fresh, still hot from the oven."

"That sounds good to me. Joe how about you?"

"Same for me."

"Two specials," yelled Meg toward the kitchen. "Drinks?" she asked.

"Sweet iced tea," said Dawn.

"Coffee, black," said Joe.

Meg left.

"Joe, I talked to my CO. He'd like to talk to you Saturday about a job. I'll pick you up Saturday morning to take you to Muroc." Dawn's face was ear-to-ear grin. "I'm so excited about this."

"That sounds swell." Joe took a deep breath and looked at her. "Dawn, there's something I have to tell you, and I don't know how to do it." Joe's careful rehearsal went out the window.

"I never told you how I ended up in Ft. Glenn I've never told anybody. I was sent there because I was cracking up at MAAF." He looked down at the table. "Captain Rogers shipped me to Alaska to get me out of the way."

"What happened?"

"It was the crash that killed Mary. It wasn't an accident." He heard Dawn's sharp breath. "I didn't remove the service plugs from the engine." He choked back a sob.

Dawn put her hand over Joe's. "People make mistakes."

"Dawn, it wasn't a mistake. I left them on purpose."

"On purpose!"

Joe watched Dawn struggle to understand. Her face darkened. "You killed Mary on purpose!" she screeched as she rose.

"I didn't… I didn't meant for that crash to happen. It was supposed to be a minor incident!"

"You bastard!" The fury in her face stung worse than the sharp slap she delivered.

Joe reached toward her. "Dawn I need to explain," he cried.

She spun away from him and fled.

He was frozen. Dawn's retreating back was an afterimage burned into his brain. It was his worst fear realized, and it was overwhelming.

He wasn't able to hold back the tears as he covered his face with his hands.

Meg's voice broke through. "Do you still want these?"

Through blurred eyes, Joe saw her holding the two plates. He shook his head, left five dollars on the table, and walked stiffly out the door and toward his room.

Through tear filled eyes, Dawn saw the lights of the guardhouse at Muroc. The guard checked her badge and waved her on to her barracks. The betrayal was crushing. The memory of that conversation she'd overheard grew like a storm cloud. And now, someone she liked, could have loved, was a part of that murder. Betrayed to the core! Tears flowed freely. How could she have been so stupid? She should have seen it. She never should have freed the rein on her heart. She wailed at the pain, howled at the frustration. This would not stand.

Joe stared at the dust swirling across the dusk-lit desert. What had he done? His mind went numb. When he looked out again, it was dark. How much time had passed? In the lobby, he called Dawn. Her roommate, Allison, answered.

"Joe, she doesn't want to talk to you. She hasn't told me what this is about, but she hasn't stopped crying since she got back."

"Allison, tell her I'll call her in the morning. I have to talk to her. I have to explain."

Joe tried to call three times on Friday, five times on Saturday, and three times on Sunday. The response was the same.

"Allison, will she ever talk to me?"

"I don't know. She's been like a clam. She goes to work, talks to no one and comes back here. I have to remind her to eat. Maybe, given time."

"Allison, tell her I have to leave. I need to get a job so I'm going back to Pasadena on the Monday bus. I'll write."

The ride to Pasadena was the longest he'd ever taken.

Chapter 14

Joe wandered around Southern California in a fog deeper than those in Ft Glenn. When his money ran low, he started looking for work. Hughes Aircraft in Culver City was hiring aircraft mechanics. They were glad to have him. Working with radical designs and new aircraft was exciting. They actually listened to his suggestions. Work kept his mind off the disaster with Dawn.

Mrs. O'Malley's rooming house was almost home. It was near the bus stop to work. It was cheap and convenient. She had grilled Joe about who he was and his work history before accepting him as a boarder.

His upstairs room was clean and neat – wood floor, flowered wallpaper, and lacy curtains. He had a small desk and a single bed. ("No female company in your room," admonished Mrs. O'Malley, index finger raised). She served breakfast promptly at six-thirty and dinner at six. If he wanted a sack lunch, she'd fix him some sandwiches.

Pasadena wasn't a good town for him. Car dealerships were popping up, but he didn't have enough money for a car. Being a working man's town, there were a lot of bars, but he wasn't much of a bar person. Mostly, Joe brought his bottle home.

He smiled to himself. The modicum of joy was the movie industry. It was always doing something. When he had time, he'd watch some of the shoots, but ordinarily it was days of eat, sleep, and work blurred together. True to his word, he wrote letters to Dawn. He wrote at night before going to bed, alone in his room with the just the radio and a scotch. It was keeping hope alive.

At first, he tried to explain what had happened and apologize. As time went on, he talked about his rooming house, his work at Hughes. Sometimes the letters were only a few lines long, but other times they would run on for several pages. No replies ever arrived, but that didn't stop him from writing.

From the hall phone he placed his usual Saturday night call. "Hi, Allison, it's Joe."

"Hey, Joe. Let me get Dawn."

Joe held his breath. Maybe this time she'd talk to him.

"Nope, she won't talk to you. Sorry."

"Thanks for trying, Allison. Talk to you next week. Goodbye." The ritual would continue for at least another week.

The following Saturday marked the end to a brutal week. The new plane project had quirks. The wing had to be redesigned, which meant the wing struts had to be altered. The crew had poured themselves into the task, trying to meet the original schedule. The workday extended into the work night for the whole week. It was finally done, and they all were exhausted. Joe hurried from the bus stop, anxious to get to his room. The bottle tucked under his arm was calling to him, offering him peace and quiet.

He started up the stairs at the boarding house. At first, the person standing on the porch didn't register. She moved in front of him, blocking his path. When he looked at her face, he froze.

"Hello, Joe. Whatta ya know?"

"Wha…" His knees weakened. He had to sit on the steps to compose himself. The paper bag with his scotch thumped onto the wooden step. With his mouth open, he watched her sit beside him. He still couldn't speak.

She looked into his eyes and said, "We have work to do."

Words formed in his mind, but his mouth refused to move. At last, he choked out, "You're here."

She laughed.

Chapter 15

Joe turned his head so she wouldn't see the tears forming. He took a deep breath. He had dreamed about a moment like this. It was here, now he was unsure what to do. He wiped his eyes, looked back at her, vision blurred. The face before him and his mental image merged. Perfect. Her blue eyes pulled at him, he was scared to let go. She quickly looked away, her ponytail swishing near his face.

Dawn turned back and touched his hand. "Joe, I've done a lot of thinking since I last saw you. I understand you were under orders. It took a while to get over the feeling of betrayal. I realized I care for you. I now see that you regret what happened, and you never meant for Mary to die. It took a lot for me to come out here to see you.

"I have to find out who was behind this campaign of sabotage against the WASP." That's what pushed me into coming. Her jaw tightened.

"Mary's incident wasn't the only one, though most of the others weren't fatal." She squeezed his hands. "Will you help me?" she implored.

Dazed from the shock of seeing her, Joe let the question hang in the air. So many thoughts raced around his head. It was a mental traffic jam.

"You wanna get something to eat?" she asked. That question brought him back.

"Yeah, sure. Let me go clean up. You want to come inside?"

"It's nice out here. I'll wait on the porch."

As Joe stood, he watched her sit in the swing like a little girl, flowered skirt and white blouse billowing as she swung back and forth.

His mind awhirl, he raced up the stairs determined to be back in less than five minutes. "Mrs. O'Malley, I'm going out for dinner," he called passing the kitchen door. Dawn rose as he walked onto the porch. A light sweater over one arm, she took his arm with her other.

"Wow, quick shower. You clean up pretty good. Where to?" she asked.

They descended the stairs into the best evening he could remember. He wanted to skip down the sidewalk. His heart was pounding so hard, she surely could hear it. The diner where he ate when he wanted a break from the boarding house fare was only three blocks away. Mrs. O'Malley's meals were regular and filling, but you could tell the day of the week by what was on the table. Monday was spaghetti and meat balls, Friday was fish, tonight was meatloaf. The peace of the evening and the joy of being with Dawn filled him.

"This is a nice neighborhood. How long have you lived here?"

He was struck by the music of her voice. "About six months." he muttered. "I knocked around for a month until my money ran out."

"It seems much longer than that since you left Mojave. I cancelled your interview with Captain Arnold at Muroc." Dawn paused, frowned and looked away from him. In a quiet voice she continued. "Joe, you devastated me when you told me about the sabotage of Mary's plane. I hated you.

I felt as if you had lied to me, betrayed me. I wanted you to go to jail.

"At first, I just threw your letters out, but you were so persistent. I started reading them, but I couldn't make myself write back. Luckily, Allison saved them all. It was your early letters that helped me understand you were an unwilling part of a greater conspiracy." Dawn touched his hand. "You had to follow orders. I won't say it wasn't your fault, but the people I want to make pay are those above you. Will you help?" she implored.

Joe was silent. They entered the railroad diner car. It was mounted on a foundation and had an attached kitchen. The wooden sign above the door simply said 'Eats.' The paint was faded and flaking, the floor was plywood.

Being a regular, he waved at Sal. Her eyes flicked over Dawn. She was the first woman he'd ever brought there. He guided Dawn to the only vacant booth of the five. The counter was full of the usual locals who politely didn't stare.

Sal appeared at the table before they sat down, coffee pot and cups in hand. "Hey, Joe." She eyed

Dawn then looked back at him. "Special tonight is turkey and potatoes. It's pretty good." She pointed at the blackboard showing the daily fare. "Drinks?"

"Just coffee," Dawn said.

"Same for me, Sal." She filled the two cups and left.

"How's the fried chicken?" asked Dawn.

"It's not as good as Melba's," he answered, "but okay. The soup is usually good, and the fish is always fresh. They have good pies here."

"Okay, fish and chips and apple pie for me."

"You want soup?" Dawn shook her head. He raised a finger and caught Sal's attention. She came over ready to refill their untouched coffees.

"The lady will take the fish and chips, and I'll have a bowl of the vegetable soup and the turkey."

Sal nodded and asked Dawn, "You want a salad?"

"No, thank you." Sal left.

Dawn traced circles on the table with her finger. "Joe, somebody ordered Mary's murder, and I want them to pay. The more I thought about it, the more I knew it wasn't you. This crime included the investigating team, and that was high up. There's one thing I haven't told anybody else." She glanced around to see if anybody was listening.

In a low voice, she continued. "After the crash, I was sitting in a dark office in the HQ. I just wanted a quiet place with nobody around. The Captain came in and went to his office. I picked up the phone to call Mary's mom, but somebody was already on the line. I don't know why, but I listened in. He called Major Williams. Do you know who he is?"

Joe thought, shrugged. "Never heard of him."

"Captain Rogers spoke about setting up the investigation to rule 'Pilot error' as the cause. He said things about getting women out of flying. Williams assured him the investigation outcome would not be questioned. It was clear that the crash was no accident.

"They also spoke about you. Captain Rogers was worried. They agreed to watch you, and if problems arose, post you somewhere out of the way."

Joe was silent. She had only confirmed what he already knew. The feeling of helplessness began to creep back into him. This time he wouldn't give in.

"I was a liability. I started drinking and making mistakes. I could've gotten somebody else killed. As much as I hate to say it, they may have saved my life. My nightmares were so intense that I hadn't slept in days. The pint of scotch before bedtime only made the visions worse. I was thinking of eating a bullet."

"Oh, Joe." Dawn squeezed his hand.

They sat quietly for a few moments until the clatter of plates on the table broke the spell. He swallowed tears and stuffed a bite of turkey in his mouth, his eyes downcast. They ate in silence. His meal was tasteless.

"Something wrong with the turkey?" asked Sal.

"Nah. I just lost my appetite."

"You want some pie? The cherry is real good."

"I'll take the cherry pie," said Dawn, pulling Sal's attention away from him. "The fish and chips was delicious."

Sal turned away.

Dawn leaned close to him. "Are you going to be okay?"

"I get these moments sometimes. It just has to run its course."

"Here's what I thought. If you come back out to Muroc, I'll get you an interview with Captain Arnold. With your background and experience at Hughes, it won't be a problem getting you on, Joe. We can work together if you're out there with me. We have to do this or you'll never be free."

"I'll never be free of it, but it is the right thing to do. I don't have any idea of how to go about investigating this."

"Me either."

Dawn's pie came, and he asked for more coffee. His mind started going down unfamiliar paths. The first thing they'd have to do is track down Captain Rogers and Major Williams.

Dawn's voice broke into his thoughts. "I've started putting together a list of incidences involving WASPs. They started early in 1944 after Gen. Hap Arnold asked the Deputy Chief of the Air Staff for permission to commission WASPs directly as Service Pilots."

He nodded. He met several commissioned civilians in Marana. Commissioning was routinely done with male civilian pilots in the Air Transport Command.

Dawn continued. "The Comptroller General of the Army Air Forces ruled against these practices. Then Jackie Cochran and General Hap Arnold went back to Congress to make the WASP a women's service within the U.S. Army Air Force. Action on this had been tabled since 1941."

He had ignored politics, so this was news to him.

"Though some of the investigations of WASP incidents indicated sabotage, all were represented to Congress as incompetence by women pilots. The bill was defeated in Congress by 19 votes, despite vigorous lobbying efforts. By the end of the 1944, the WASP were disbanded – sent home, without any benefits. We didn't even get transportation costs – just told to go away."

Surprise showed on Joe's face. "Gosh, even I got transportation pay. I remembered in Marana, you called other WASP to send money to ship Mary's body home. I contributed."

Dawn continued, "Those are the general facts, but I need help investigating the details, and I need a lot of help tracking down those involved. Do you think we can do it?"

His coffee was cold. He signaled Sal for a fresh cup. "If we're going to start this, we need to get things straight. I'm not sure my being at Muroc will help us. I mean Muroc is not the best place to conduct an investigation. It might help us, that is you and me, but not…"

"Yeah, I understand," Dawn said. "I can probably contact other WASPs, start listing things that happened, and maybe get someone started tracking down Williams and Rogers. But after that, Muroc is isolated."

He looked at her. "That was my thought, too. I don't have any time off yet, but I could go on night shift so I could do things during the day. What we really need is a friend in Records. I have an old high-school pal who's still in the service, a clerk in Army Records. We haven't stayed in touch much, but I did get an occasional letter from him while I was in Alaska. He managed to track me down even there. I'll have to think how to approach him about this. He could get his ass in a sling."

"If he knew what this was about, would he still help?" asked Dawn.

"He's career, so I'm not sure. We'll start out with a story of me wanting to get in touch with some old buddies. I think I better save the real reason for a face-to-face visit. Are you staying over tonight, or heading back?"

"I came to Pasadena with Allison. She has family here she's visiting, She's going to pick me up later."

Silence filled the air. "Dawn, I was getting pretty sweet on you before. If you are only interested in this project of yours, that's okay, but I need to know." He couldn't get his hopes up. His heart couldn't take another blow.

Concern crossed her face. She paused. "Joe, I care for you, let's take it slow. Allison's going to pick me up at nine-thirty. She can drop me off again tomorrow, but we need to leave by two-o'clock. We have to be back at work Monday."

He looked at his watch. It was nine-o'clock, which meant it was after midnight in D. C. – too late to call Dennis. He'd do it in the morning.

"Is it late?" asked Dawn.

"Not really but let's walk back." They got up. He put five dollars on the table.

Chapter 16

The night was clear with a warm breeze coming over the mountains. He understood this was a precursor to the Santa Ana Winds. A few people were out walking, sitting on porches, chatting over the fences. It was a nice evening. He tried to enjoy the stroll, but so much was crowding into his mind.

Until Dawn showed up, he didn't understand that resolving this was something he had to do. Now, there was no doubt. As surely as he had to take the next breath, Joe had to see this through. He wanted to be with Dawn, but getting this crime exposed was a matter of life or death for him.

Dawn and Joe paused at the bottom of his rooming house steps. "You'll help me?" she asked picking imaginary lint from his sleeve.

Joe sighed and turned to her. "I owe it to you. I owe it to Mary. I have to confront this, to expose it. Yes, I'm going to help. I'll call Dennis tomorrow just to chat. I might go there, I have comp time coming from the doubles I've been working."

"I put a little money away. My roommate, Allison, was a WASP too, so she'll help. I haven't told her anything about this yet, but …"

"I have enough for my train fare," Joe interrupted. "Allison will have to know sometime. What do you think her reaction will be?"

"She'll be as outraged as I am," Dawn growled.

"What about her feelings toward me, what I did? How will she take that?" Joe whispered.

"She'll want to get to the bottom of this, just like we do. She'll accept that you never meant to hurt anyone."

"Joe, Allison's here." She pointed at the Desoto pulling to the curb. "I'll come back tomorrow, and we can figure out what to do next."

Dawn gave him a peck on the cheek and walked to the car. She turned and waved. His hand rose. His cheek burned.

The morning had been nice, the weather beautiful. He and Dawn walked around and mostly stayed away from the topic of sabotage. Reaching the boarding house, it couldn't be ignored any longer. "Let's call Dennis," said Joe.

The phone rang twice. "Sergeant Lardner's residence. Billy speaking."

Joe was taken aback by the formality of the young voice. "This is Sergeant Clark. May I speak to your father?"

"Yes sir. I'll get him." There was a shout, "Dad, phone for you. It's Sergeant Clark."

There was a fumbling noise. "Joe! I haven't heard from you in ages. How the hell are ya? Where are ya?"

"Hi, Dennis. I'm fine. After Alaska, I moved to California. If I never see another snowflake, it will be too soon. I don't even use ice in my scotch." They both laughed.

"So you decided to make a career out of the Army?" Joe asked. His stomach began to knot.

"Yeah, they treat me pretty good. Unlike you, I don't have aircraft mechanic skills. The world's full of clerks, so I'm going to keep doing what I'm doing and put in my twenty.

"That was a rough break you got. I never was able to find out why you got posted to Alaska. Maybe you can tell me the story over dinner."

Joe hesitated. "I'll wrangle time off to come visit."

"Sure, anytime. What are you doing now?" Dennis asked.

"I'm working at Hughes Aircraft in Culver City doing the same thing I was doing for the Army – aircraft maintenance. The planes are a lot hotter, though."

"Wow! I've heard rumors about some of the things they're doing," Dennis exclaimed. "When could ya get back here?"

Here it was. Once he started a schedule, he was committed. "I'll check on what the situation is at work. I have a little time off, and things are getting slow. They might let me take a couple of weeks. I'll get back to you as soon as I find out anything."

"Great talking to ya, Joe. Look forward to seeing ya. You'll get to see Jacqui and the family.

Jacqui's as gorgeous as ever, and Billy's really grown."

"I'm looking forward to it. See you soon. I'll call with my schedule when I get it together. Bye, Dennis."

Joe hung up the phone. Part of him was relieved to have acted at last, but another part was nervous. "I don't know if I can be straight with Dennis. If this sabotage against the WASP goes up high enough, he could jeopardize his career. I'd like to believe the service still has honor and wrongs get righted, but…"

Dawn sensed his nervousness. She felt a little guilty, like she was using him, but she was also pushing Joe to resolve this crisis in his life. "Joe, Allison wants to leave this afternoon so we can get back before dark. Want to go to a movie?"

"You mean like a date? Sure! I don't know much about movies. What do you want to see?"

"There's a new one out called *The Razor's Edge* that's supposed to be pretty good."

"Yeah, that's on the marquee at the theater around the corner. Let's get some lunch and go."

Chapter 17

Joe hesitated then dialed Dawn's number. The phone rang twice. "Hello, Allison Chambers here."

"Hi, Allison, it's Joe. Could I speak to Dawn."

"Hi-de-ho, Joe. Soitently. I'll get her for ya," her voice lively.

Joe laughed. Allison did that to him.

Dawn cleared her throat. "Hey, Joe. Whaddya know."

"Hi, Dawn. I talked to my boss today, and with a slowdown coming and the holiday, he was glad to give me a couple of weeks off without pay. Dennis is looking forward to seeing me in Washington. I can catch the train from here tomorrow night and be in Washington on Friday. Dennis says he'll meet me. He's trying to get me into the visiting Non-Commissioned Officers quarters. That'll help stretch my bucks a bit."

"Are you jake with this?" Dawn asked.

Joe sighed. He knew it was the right decision. "Dawn, It's something I have to do."

"Joe, I want to see you off. I'll ask Allison if I can borrow her car. I can take you to the train station and save you the cab fare."

"Dawn, I want to see you too, but it's a long trip for a weekday. I can take the bus."

"Okay, if that's what you want. Call me."

"At every opportunity. I'm missing you already. Bye."

"Bye, Joe. Be careful."

The die was cast. He felt as if he were already on a train heading toward… he didn't know what. One thing was certain. This was the onset of major changes in his life. A chasm of the unknown opened before him.

Chapter 18

Joe looked out the window at the depot in Yuma. This was his first train ride since discharge. The train left late last night, so everybody slept. As it descended the pass, the sun was coming up over the desert.

Yuma was only slightly better than Mojave. It did have the Colorado River close, but not much else. Joe got out to walk around, stretch his legs a bit. He wasn't the only passenger strolling about. He nodded at several.

How was he going to approach Dennis? What information was he was seeking? What was he going to do with what he found out? That was the big one. Dawn and he didn't have a clear goal.

I have to feel Dennis out, he thought. He could use the excuse he was just looking for his old CO. Dennis would accept that if it were done in an offhand manner. He'd have to find out where Captain Rogers and Major Williams are now.

To find out more about WASP incidences, I'm going to have to level with Dennis, he thought. Things could change. What's Dennis's present assignment? What access does he have to records? So many questions. What if he might choose not to help? Joe felt guilty using him, but what else could he do?

Thinking about this too was giving him a headache. He should've brought a book, he thought. He'd find one at the next stop. He looked out the window. The scenery wasn't interesting for long stretches. After crossing the Rockies, there were vistas of flat land, empty land. It was easy to imagine he was alone in that vast countryside – nobody to bother him. Then Dawn's image appeared, and he'd ach for her.

He hoped Dawn was getting stuck on him. How would he feel about that if she were? He loved her, he decided – wanted to spend the rest of his life with her. A picture of them in that white cottage with the picket fence and kids running around formed. His lips curled into a smile.

Then a dose of reality intruded. Would he still be working at Hughes? Would he take a job at Muroc? Would they both work there? Would Dawn quit her job to become a mom? She seemed pretty keen about her work. He had to quit thinking about all that for a while. The questions were overwhelming him.

Time dragged on, seeming to move slower than the train. Maybe it was just that he was impatient and wanted to get this nightmare resolved and out of his mind. It would be nice to see Dennis and gab about old times.

Joe stopped a porter. "How long to D. C.?" he asked

"Washington D. C. in one hour," announced the porter

In the bathroom, he splashed water on his face, washing the sleep from his eyes and the weariness from his face.

The train slowed. "Union Station" cried the porter.

He saw Dennis on the platform as the train stopped. People crowded the aisles, grabbing their bags, moving toward the door.

Joe could wait a few minutes for it to clear. He watched Dennis examine each departing passenger. Married life sure agreed with Dennis. He'd put on at least twenty pounds. Stepping onto the platform, Joe walked toward him. Dennis hadn't seen him yet.

"Sergeant Lardner, straighten up that gig line." Dennis turned toward Joe, puzzlement on his face. A smile broke out. They hugged with a lot of back slapping. It had been a long time.

"Long trip, Joe?" he asked.

"It sure seemed to drag at times, but here I am. Let me get my duffle, and we can get out of here."

Dennis held the door of the red Plymouth open for Joe.

"Nice car," remarked Joe.

"It's only a couple of years old. I bought it from a lieutenant in my office. With the family and everything, we needed a car. You got one?"

"Nope, I'm still walking and riding the bus. Can't afford one yet."

"I got you into the visiting NCO quarters on base, so let's drop your gear. We can have lunch at the NCO Club. I want to catch up with everything."

The NCO club was no different from the others Joe had visited, busy at lunchtime. Once seated, he let Dennis do most of the talking. It gave Joe a chance to read him, figure out how to broach the subject of Captain Rogers and the WASP.

Dennis liked clerking in records, and with the end of the war, a lot of clerking was needed. His position seemed secure – important to a family man. Washington D. C. was the hub of government, and Dennis looked sharp. His uniform was neat, his round face held a healthy glow. He swallowed the last bite of his hamburger. "Joe, you've let me ramble on. What about you? What's happening?"

"After I got back stateside, I knocked around Southern California for a while before taking a job with Hughes Aircraft. I tell ya, Dennis, they got some radical new designs. And those things are fast! We're hearing rumors about a new aircraft under development, the American version of the German Messerschmitt 262. It'll make the prop obsolete." He wanted to talk about anything but the real purpose of his visit.

"Wow!" exclaimed Dennis.

He continued, "The ME 262 came out too late to make a difference in the war. There weren't a lot of them, but that plane scared our guys bad. They came back from the bombing runs rattled. After VE, day there was a scramble to get the German planes and engineers into the U.S. Rumor has it everything went to Dayton and Muroc."

Dennis rubbed his chin. "I've seen invoices with the same cost center coming from both those places for something called 'jet engines,' whatever those are."

"Yeah, it's all pretty hush-hush. I may try to get hired on there. It sounds exciting."

Dennis looked at him. "Met anyone?"

Whew! Here it was. How far to go? Joe's stomach tightened. He stopped himself from squirming in his seat.

"Actually, I have. She's living in Muroc, working as a mechanic."

"A woman mechanic! Working at Muroc! No wonder you're looking to get on there." He laughed. "Where'd you meet her?"

"I first met her while stationed at Marana Army Air Field. She and another WASP flew in to pick up a couple of planes we'd overhauled." He needed to change the subject. "Speaking of Marana, Dennis, can you help me find my old CO from Marana? His name was Captain Allen Rogers." Joe watched his eyes, searching for signs of discomfort at his question. He saw none.

"Is he still in the service?" Dennis asked, finishing the last of his French fries.

Joe shrugged. "I completely lost track when I went to Ft. Glenn."

Dennis smiled. "Tomorrow's Friday. A lot of people are getting a head start on the Labor Day weekend. Let me show you around my office in the morning. We could take a quick look. If his files are at Myers, I could do a little office work while you look at them. Nobody will be there."

He pushed his chair back and stood. "Let's get outta here. Jacqui's looking forward to seeing you, and with this weather, we can sit in the yard with some Pabst BRs. We'll grill steaks. That is, if you're not too tired."

Chapter 19

Family housing at Myers was nice. Dennis and Jacqui had worked within their limited budget to make it homey. Family life agreed with Jacqui. Not the skinny girl Joe remembered, she had flowered into the all-American home keeper. She met them at the door wearing a flared skirt and white blouse. Her now-blond hair was in twin ponytails. Her arms flew around his neck.

"Joe, it's been so long. Welcome to our home." From behind her, a four-year-old peeked out. "This is Billy."

Joe held out his hand to shake. Billy's small hand slowly reached around his mom. "I spoke to you on the phone a few nights ago. Do you remember?" He nodded as Joe shook his hand.

"Honey, Joe and I are going to the back yard. How about a couple of beers?"

The back yard was neat, grass mowed and trimmed, rose bushes lining one side, a picnic table and barbeque on the patio. "This is really nice. No wonder you want to be a lifer." Joe was envious. Dennis was living his dream.

The screen door slammed as Billy handed them their beers. He now had on a cowboy hat and holster with his cap gun handy. Joe locked that scene into his memory. Jacqui joined them at the table as Billy ran around wiping out imaginary foes with the popping of his cap gun.

"Joe's got a girl in California," said Dennis. "She's an aircraft mechanic."

Jacqui's mouth opened then closed as she processed this information. "What's her name?"

He was reluctant to bring Dawn into this, but now he had to. "Dawn. I met her while at Marana. She was a pilot."

"Wow! A pilot, a female pilot. How did that happen?" asked Jacqui.

"During the war, male pilots were needed overseas, so women with pilot's licenses were recruited to fly domestically. They were called

Women's Airforce Service Pilots, W.A.S.P for short. Dawn was one of those."

"Gee, imagine that. Is anything going to come of it?" she asked with a smile.

Joe looked down, breaking eye contact. "Too soon to tell. I'll let you know."

"Dennis said you had it pretty rough in Alaska. What happened?"

Dennis interrupted, "Jacqui, let's not put him under the third degree on his first day here."

"They needed me up there, so that's where I went. Later I'll tell you more about life at Fort Glenn, or lack thereof." They laughed.

"Jacqui, let's get dinner going. Joe's been on a train for three days."

She went to the kitchen to get things ready while Dennis started the barbeque with a whoosh and leaping flames.

"Tomorrow I want to hear the story of why you got posted to that hellhole. Tonight we eat, drink, and make merry. Billy, go get Uncle Joe and me another beer."

They ate outside and watched the lightning bugs greet the night. Joe hadn't seen sparkles like that in years. Billy chased them with a jar until Jacqui announced bedtime. He took in the scene. Someday… ?

Joe's weariness showed. Dennis bundled him into the car and took him back to the NCO quarters.

"I'll pick you up at 07:00. We'll get breakfast before heading to my office. Sleep well, my friend."

Joe waved at the departing car.

The visiting Non Commissioned Officers quarters were quiet, most visitors having gone home for the holiday. Despite his exhaustion, sleep eluded him. He felt as if he were alone, sticking his neck out. He missed Dawn, missed her guidance about how to approach Dennis. And Jacqui had honed in on him like a P-51 on a strafing run.

Watching Dennis and his family made him want to drop this investigation with its risks and build a life with Dawn. But it would be a burr under both their saddles. So, he'd go with the story of wanting to find his old buddies. It would work for a while. If he could hold off the story of Fort Glenn until after he looked at the files, he'd come away with something. He knew he couldn't lie, Dennis would see through it.

What were they going to do with any information Joe got? That depended on what he found out and…

When he was with Dawn, everything seemed clear. He'd call her tomorrow. He needed to hear her voice. Sleep finally came.

Joe exited the barracks as Dennis pulled up, right on time. He had stopped at a donut shop. They had breakfast with the fresh pot of coffee Dennis made at his office. With the long weekend, the place was deserted, everybody coupling leave with the holiday.

Dennis showed him the system and found Captain Rogers file on the third try. He left Joe while he did some work. One thing the army was good at was organization. Though the number of files was massive, things could be located.

Joe sat at a table, the gooseneck lamp a pool of light in the warehouse of file cabinets. Captain Rogers was still in the Army, a major now. He was an assistant to Lt. Colonel Jake Williams, both assigned to Washington. Joe's heart sped up. He worked right here in Washington. He scribbled down information so he could find Rogers.

Jake Williams' file took Joe a while to find. He set it on the table next to Rogers' file. He looked at them. Again, doubt arose over what he and Dawn would do with the information. Maybe they would do nothing, he thought. Without that information they couldn't make a choice. He opened William's file and read.

Both he and the Captain had been promoted and assigned to Colonel Ted Marshall in the Inspector General's Office. Joe shook his head. This was so wrong.

From Col. Marshall's file, Joe took notes on the six officers assigned to him since the end of the war. Further checking revealed all had been in aircraft maintenance or incident investigation. The gang was together. He made notes as fast as he could.

"Lunchtime," echoed Dennis's voice.

"Let me return these files," said Joe.

"You can do that after we eat," said Dennis. "I'm hungry."

Back at the NCO Club Dennis asked, "Find what you were looking for?"

Joe nodded. "I might look up Cap… Major Rogers while I'm here."

"If you need my car, say the word," Dennis said around a mouthful of fried chicken. "Tomorrow's Saturday. Wanna see some sights?"

Joe wanted a little distance from what he'd found out. "How about the Capitol and Lincoln Memorial? I'd like to see those while I'm here."

"You got a lot more to do?" asked Dennis.

"Naw, just tidy up."

"Good, because Jacqui's expecting you for dinner."

Dinner at the Lardner's was pot-roast. Jacqui was a good cook, whirling around the kitchen in her apron, humming to herself. She laid out the table. As they said Grace, Joe watched Billy squirm. The food was delicious. After his third helping, Joe waved Jacqui's hovering hand away.

"Saved room for dessert, I hope," she smiled. "I made rhubarb pie. It's Aunt Ellie's recipe. She always said it was your favorite." Jacqui smiled. "Your Aunt Ellie was so helpful while I was carrying Billy. Everybody else shunned me. How is she?"

Joe hung his head. "I haven't talked with her since Dennis and I enlisted. I wrote, but she never wrote back. I kept sending my pay to them throughout the war. You know how they needed it. I never heard anything. I guess I just let it slip."

"Joe, your aunt can't write. You know that."

"But all of us kids were in school. She made sure of that. They can read and write. Anyway, I'll get in touch with her. I promise."

The pie was as good as aunt Ellie's.

"Joe, I want to know more about this girl you're seeing," said Jacqui

Joe's mind raced. This was dangerous ground. Dennis would want to know more about his Alaska assignment too.

"I first met Dawn when she came to Marana to pick up a plane we overhauled. After she left, I wrote her some, and she wrote back. It wasn't anything serious. She told me she was working at a base in Southern California, so I thought I'd visit her when I got back to the States. I did see her, but we had a few problems, so I went back to Pasadena and found a job."

"You're not seeing her now?" asked Jacqui.

Joe shrugged. "I don't know if I could get serious about her. She's keen about her job." Joe looked at Dennis. He looked like he was biting his lip at Jacqui's inquisition.

"Joe, you need to find someone. I have some friends here…"

Dennis couldn't hold back his laugher. "Jacqui, give the poor boy a rest."

Joe needed to think, to figure out what to tell Dennis and how to do it. He had to talk to Dawn, so he begged weariness.

Dennis dropped him off with a promise to pick him up at 09:00 hours.

Dawn was waiting for his call, answering right away. He told her he'd found Rogers and Williams still in the Army and stationed in Washington. He also explained what he'd found about Marshall and others who might be involved. Somehow, the incident reports had to be checked to see whose names were on them. He'd have to open up to Dennis to get his help.

"Joe, I have some information too," Dawn said. "I talked to several of the WASP about incidents of possible sabotage. I have a list. Only three involved fatalities, one of those was Mary."

He wrote down the places and the dates.

"Our network is good, Joe. Some of those involved are going to take pictures of their logbooks with *their* accounts of what happened."

It was all she could give him until the logbook photos came.

"Dawn, what are we going to do with this information? Where are we going?"

"We're going to expose them, of course! They deserve to be punished. They murdered people, my sisters," she yelled into the phone.

Her vehemence startled Joe. "You're right. That's what we're going to do." He wasn't nearly as sure as he sounded. They had little hard evidence, and these people were powerful.

"I sure wish you were here," he said. "Tomorrow we're going on a family outing around D. C. with a picnic at the Jefferson Memorial. After that, I'll have to tell Dennis what happened and what we're doing. It's the only way we can access more records."

There was only the hiss of the phone in his ear.

"Joe, I wish I were there too, but I'm getting information through the WASP network from here. Some of the other gals want to just let sleeping dogs lie. I can't. I was there."

The only sound was the hiss.

"I'm missing you a lot." He had nothing else to say.

"I miss you too, Joe. Call me."

Chapter 20

It was a gorgeous late summer day in Washington. Visiting the Jefferson and Lincoln Memorial affected Joe. These men founded and believed in the nation, in people having the ability to govern themselves. They stood up for what was right. It stiffened his resolve to go ahead.

Billy ran out of energy about three, and they packed their basket and blanket. Joe carried the sleeping cowboy to the car. Dinner at the Lardner's was simple leftovers and tomato soup. Jacqui took Billy to bed. Dennis and he were alone in the back yard, beers in hand. Joe was quiet, apprehensive over what was to come.

The moment of truth had arrived.

Dennis looked at him. "What happened that ended up with you in Umnak? It has the worst weather in the world, one of the most Godforsaken places on Earth. People are sent there for a reason."

With his hands folded on the table, Joe told Dennis the story without looking at him once. He choked back sobs several times while describing the crash and Mary's death.

A look of sympathy crossed Dennis's face. Now he understood why Joe was posted to Alaska. He shook his head.

"Dawn is the other WASP pilot who was in Marana?" he asked. Joe nodded. "And the two of you are going to do what?"

"Dawn wants to expose this whole dirty scheme."

"What about you? What do you want to do?"

"I want the burning in my soul to go away! Time has not healed this wound."

"So you're doing this for yourself and for Dawn?"

Joe nodded.

Dennis stared hard at Joe. "I'm going to throw cold water on this plan. First, I can't help you anymore. The Army is my career. When it's discovered I helped you, at the least, I'll be given a dishonorable discharge. They could prosecute me as a spy, releasing confidential records." He shook his head. "So, no. No more from me. Just your visit will bring me under suspicion.

"Second, these people have power. They can do what it takes to keep this quiet if they're threatened." His voice rose. "You've already put me and my family at risk. If you move forward, everything I've spent my life building will be lost."

Fury showed in his face. "I'm taking you to the train station tomorrow. I don't want to hear from you again. Bury this, Joe, for everybody's sake." Dennis stood. "Let's go back to the NCO quarters. I'll make excuses to Jacqui why you had to leave. Don't do this, Joe."

The next morning, Dennis made one last run at him to change his mind on the drive to Union Station. "Are you going foreword with this?"

"I don't know. I'll talk to Dawn when I get back." Doubt showed on Dennis's face that they'd drop it. "Are you going to say anything about our investigation?"

He didn't answer.

If Dawn agreed to drop it, no harm done. If not, to protect himself, Dennis had to report it. He'd still face the violation of letting Joe into the facility, even if Joe said he only toured, that he did not look at any records. That story was weak. The drive and Joe's departure were icy after that.

Joe was worried. He'd call Dawn at the next stop, tell her he was on his way back. The rest must wait until they were together.

An hour into the trip, the greenery of Virginia rolled by, but he didn't notice. His conscience was torn over the murder, losing Dawn if he quit, and ruining his friend's and his family's life. There was no good answer, no good option.

Joe called during the stop at Richmond. The phone rang twice before Dawn picked up. "Dawn, I'm on my way back. I'll be there Wednesday."

"Joe, what happened?"

"It didn't go well with Dennis. I'll tell you about it when I get back. I did get addresses for Rogers and Williams. Their boss, Marshall, may have been involved along with others. There's not much time before the train leaves, so let's talk about that later."

"Whatever you say, Joe. The photos of the logbooks should be in the mail by the end of next week, so we'll get something from that. I'll talk to you on Wednesday."

The announcement of the train's departure rang over the sound system. "Gotta go. See you in a couple of days. Miss you."

"Miss you too, Joe. See ya. Bye."

Joe's eyes saw none of the countryside passing by the train. Joe had put Dennis in a bad position, and it wasn't fair to him. Would Dennis say anything? They both signed in when they went to the records warehouse. Joe's visit as his guest was in the log. If he were Dennis, he'd consider his family. That would make up his mind.

Not good for Dawn and Joe. A shiver ran down his back. What would those involved do? How far would they go?

Chapter 21

At the bus depot in Pasadena, Joe took a cab directly to the Hughes plant and spoke to his boss, Matt.

"Good to see you back, Joe. The new design changes are complete, so the rework starts tomorrow. I need you."

"I'll be here. I could use the paycheck."

As he walked to the bus stop, Joe wondered what hornet's nest he had poked in Washington D.C. Dennis's reaction was not what he'd hoped for, but it was understandable. What would he do now? He had to cover his ass. How much would he tell them? He got off at his normal stop, walked to the pay phone on the corner, and called Dawn.

"Hi, it's me. I've been thinking about Dennis. I think you should be cautious."

"What do you mean?" she asked, worry in her voice.

"If this comes out, the people who are involved would be hurt and are in a position to stop us. I think we should be careful, and as much as I want to see you, maybe you should stay away from me for a while. If Dennis says anything about this, he may leave you out. They'll know about only me."

"Joe, I want to see you!"

He wanted to see her, too. "Dawn, it's just for a while. We need to be sure. This could be dangerous. These people murdered Mary. From now on we'll use pay phones."

"Joe, this is scaring me." Her voice trembled.

"Me too." Joe had to be strong, reassure her. "It's probably nothing, but let's not take a chance." He gave her the number of the phone booth. She agreed to call him tomorrow at 19:00 hours. As he walked back to the rooming house, he kept glancing over his shoulder. He saw no one suspicious, but that didn't mean they weren't there.

The aroma of dinnertime greeted him as he climbed the rooming house steps. "Good evening, Mrs. O'Malley."

"I'm so glad you are back. Will you be joining us for dinner?" she asked.

"Yes, ma'am, I'd like to." He smiled at her.

"Well, have a seat there next to Johnny."

Johnny was her ten-year-old son. Joe played ball with him and gave him a glove.

He smiled up at Joe. "We kinda missed ya, Joe."

"Mister Clark," his mother corrected.

"It's fine if he wants to call me Joe."

"Mister Clark," she repeated.

He turned to Johnny. "I went back East to visit a friend of mine, Johnny."

"Was it someone you knew in the war?" he asked.

"Before the war. He and I went to school together. I was a little younger than you when we became pals, did stuff together all the time."

"Gee. That's a long time ago."

"Well, not that long ago. You want to throw the ball for a while after dinner?" he asked, changing the subject.

"Yeah!" Conversation ceased as the meatloaf was served. Mrs. O'Malley made great meatloaf.

After coffee, He and Johnny went outside. Joe knelt beside him in the grass. "Johnny there's something you can do for me."

"Sure, Mr. Clark."

"When we're together, call me Joe, Okay?"

A big smile crossed his face. "Yeah, sure."

"Johnny, if you see anybody strange nosing around, will you let me know?"

"What do ya mean 'strange'?" he asked.

"Somebody not from around here, somebody who's not from the neighborhood. And let's keep it a secret between us. Don't even tell your mom, Okay?"

"Yeah, okay," he said enthusiastically.

They threw the ball until it got dark, and Johnny's mom called bedtime. They went in and said goodnight. For the first time in his life, he looked around his room – what had changed since he was last there. Everything looked as he had left it, but he couldn't be sure. It marked the start of a change in his life.

The next morning Joe gathered all of his notes and letters from Dawn. On the way to work, he stopped at the bus station, putting everything in a locker. His room had nothing to indicate he was looking into the deaths and sabotage against the WASP, and more importantly, there was no connection to Dawn. He kept looking over his shoulder, watching the street behind him in the reflections of store windows. Nothing strange or unusual. Everything was so ordinary. Once on the job, work held his focus.

Chapter 22

Colonel Ted Marshall of the Inspector General's Office sat behind his oversized desk looking over a steaming coffee cup at Major Rogers and Lt. Colonel Williams. He cleared his throat, glancing at the photos of him with various personages of note hanging on the wall.

"Gentlemen, the reason you're here is that someone has started asking questions about a few of the incident investigations we did a few years ago. Staff Sergeant Lardner in Records allowed a former soldier access to files. Former Sergeant Joseph Clark, was released from service soon after the war and is a school friend. He asked Lardner to pull incident investigation reports involving Women Airforce Service Pilots. Lardner refused."

Major Rogers spoke. "Did you say the man's name was Joseph Clark?"

"That's correct," confirmed Colonel Marshall.

Rogers explained. "Clark was my chief mechanic at Marana Army Air Field. He assisted in an incident where a WASP was killed. Clark didn't handle it well and started to crack up. I shipped him up to Fort Glenn on Umnak Island for the duration. At first, I kept in contact with his CO, but there were no complaints, so I lost track of him."

"What was his involvement?"

"He left the service plugs in the engine of the AT- 6 they had overhauled. It wasn't supposed to be a fatality, but when the engine quit, she tried to bring the plane around to land. Every pilot knows not to do that. She burned in the wreckage, and Clark was the first one on the site. He saw it all."

"God!" exclaimed the Colonel. "What's our exposure?"

"We had the investigation team on site the next day. The finding was *'Pilot Error.'* We're covered," Williams said.

"There was another WASP on site at the time," Rogers said. "Both of them were taking AT-6s to Sweetwater training. She stayed around during the investigation, pretty broken up over the death of her friend."

"What was her name?" asked the Colonel.

"I'll pull the records. She's listed as a witness," said Lt. Colonel Alexander.

"Let's find Joe Clark and keep an eye on him. I want more information on who he socialized with at Ft. Glenn. Check with the censor boys to see who wrote letters to him, who he wrote to. I also want to find out where this other WASP is. We need to know if Clark is pursuing this on his own or if others are involved. We'll decide what to do then. I'll brief General Davidson.

"Gentlemen, use whatever resources you need. I'll expect reports in five days. Dismissed."

Chapter 23

Joe noticed the man in the bad suit the next morning as he approached the bus stop. He looked uncomfortable in his suit. He hung back from the bench pretending to read an L.A. Times. When the bus came, he got on with Joe. Military Police all the way, Joe thought. At the plant, the 'suit' got off with Joe. As Joe went through the gate, showing his badge. The man stepped into the guardhouse. This wasn't good. Joe's stomach began to knot.

At noon, his boss called him into his sty of an office, reeking of cigarettes. "Joe, there was a guy here asking about you this morning. Are you in some kind of trouble?"

He shrugged. "Don't think so, Matt. What was he asking?" Beads of sweat formed in the middle of his back. He clamped down on rising panic.

"The guy asked what you're doing for us." He stubbed his cigarette out in an overflowing ashtray. "Are you looking for another job?"

"No, I'm not. I like it here. I like you as a boss. Did he ask personal questions?"

"Yeah, but I don't know nothin' about your personal life, so I couldn't tell him anything."

"I don't understand what this guy was after, Matt. I haven't done anything wrong." Joe almost believed it himself.

"I believe ya, Joe. I hate when people come snooping around. The war's over. We did our part." He picked up his pack of Lucky Strikes, shaking one out.

"Thanks, Matt. I appreciate it." Joe left the office determined not to show how scared he was. The rest of the day was a blur.

When Joe came home that night, another 'suit' followed. Pretending to ignore him, Joe had to shake him before Dawn's call.

Johnny plopped down next to Joe at the dinner table. "Hey ya, J... Mr. Clark. Can we play some ball after dinner?"

"Sure, Johnny. Good day at school?"

"Aw, ya know."

Conversation ceased as the large bowl of beef stew arrived at the table.

After dinner, Johnny and Joe grabbed their gloves. In the corner of the yard away from the house, Johnny whispered, "Joe, there was some guys here today wantin' to check out your room. They made my mom promise not to say anything. Are you in some kinda trouble? These guys looked like G-men. You're not a spy or anything, are ya?"

"Johnny. I'm just a guy trying to make a living. I'm here. I did my part in the war."

"What about that girl who was here for you awhile back?"

He smiled at Johnny. "She's an old friend. Don't say anything to anybody about her, okay."

"Yeah sure, Joe."

"Let's throw the ball a bit before it gets dark."

When Johnny's mother called him in, it was Joe's cue to get to the phone booth. Peeking around the side of the house, he saw a car parked across the street with two shadows in it, the glow of a cigarette visible. A trembling Joe slipped out the back gate. Hurrying around the corner, he could hear the phone ringing and grabbed it. "Hello."

"Joe?" Dawn asked, a tremble in her voice..

"Yeah, it's me." He breathed a sigh of relief at the sound of her voice.

"This is the second time I called. I was worried. Are you Okay?"

"I'm fine. There's a couple of guys who've been following me all day. One talked to my boss at work today. They're outside my rooming house right now, so I had to sneak out. They talked to my landlady, wanted to search my room." He heard her sharp intake of breath.

"It's okay. There wasn't anything for them to find. I cleared out my room before they showed up. You're safe. Don't worry."

"This is giving me the heebie-jeebies. I'm scared."

Joe was scared too, but he had to be brave for her. "I think we're fine. But be careful. How much does Allison know?"

"Joe, I had to tell her what happened in Marana. I told her we were looking into some of the incidents that happened to the WASP. I didn't tell her about you. She's as mad as I am."

"Tell Allison someone's trying to block our investigation. You and she have to contact the WASP you talked to, tell them to say nothing. Get all of your notes and records out of your room. Find a secure place to store them. We'll talk more tomorrow, okay."

As Joe slipped through the back gate, he saw Mrs. O'Malley on the back porch.

"Mr. Clark, a word, if you please." They went into the kitchen.

"A couple o' gents was here today. They told me to say nothing, but something wasn't kosher about those two." She wiped her hands on her apron and crossed her arms over her ample chest. "Asking about you, they were. I only told them you had gone visiting a friend back East. They wanted to look in your room, but I wouldn't let 'em. Told them they needed a warrant, I did. What would this be about?"

"Thank you for sticking up for me. This is a problem from the war. Something bad happened. Men who were involved are trying to keep it a secret. I may have to leave."

"Mr. Clark, you've been like Johnny's father, God rest his soul. Heartbroken, he'll be if you must leave. The loss of another good man in his life would hurt him. A good man you are, Mr. Clark."

"I'm sorry about that, but it's for your protection too." He hoped his leaving would keep them out of any problems.

"When will you be goin'?"

"I don't know."

Chapter 24

Joe looked at the street with new eyes. How did this nice neighborhood become menacing? He saw only cars he recognized, no strangers lurking at the corners. At the bus stop, only the usual crowd waited. There was nothing out of the ordinary at work.

He saw no sign of the guys tailing him going home. Joe needed to talk to Dawn and went directly to the phone booth.

Allison answered. "Oh, Joe! I'm glad you called," she wailed. "I was trying to find your number. I've been frantic," she broke down in sobs. "The police showed up asking if I knew Dawn Dunham. When I said yes, they asked me to go with them. Oh, Joe!

"She borrowed my car to come see you, she had some things to show you. There's been an accident!" Her voice broke. It took her several seconds to recover. "They took me to the scene. In the pass, the car went over the side into the ravine. She was under a sheet on a stretcher. I had to identify her." She sobbed again.

"Allison! What happened? How's Dawn?" Joe screamed.

"Oh God, Joe. It was Dawn! She was…so still." Allison's voice rose to a wail.

"They were interviewing witnesses. They said some crazy driver, weaving all over the road, forced her off. The guy sped off, just leaving her. Some other guy stopped and crawled down to try to help. He found her ID. The police brought me back, they just left here." She sobbed, trying to catch her breath.

His world stopped.

"Joe, are you there? Did you hear me?"

Her voice broke through the roaring in his ears. "I'm… I'm here. I…"

"Joe, I'll call her family, but I wanted to talk to you first. Wait, there's a couple of guys in uniform coming down the hall. They're knocking on my door."

Allison's voice rang out. "Can I help you guys?"

Joe couldn't understand what was being said.

"Joe, these guys are from the government, here for Dawn's stuff. I don't understand, but I gotta go. I'll call you later."

The phone went dead. He stood staring at it, not seeing it, feeling nothing. The enormity blanked everything out. He made himself breathe.

Stumbling back home, he tripped up the steps. Mrs. O'Malley appeared at his side. Dazed, he turned toward her. She looked at him and her eyes widened.

"Joe, you look like you've seen a ghost. What's wrong?" She reached out to steady him.

"I…I just found out a friend of mine died. She…" he choked.

"Who was it, Joe? Surely not that sweet girl who was coming 'round?"

His head nodded without thought. The trauma of the news froze his brain. Part of him rejected this. It couldn't be true. He refused to let it be true. But the cold wave seeped through his disbelief.

"Oh, blessed Lord! I'm so sorry. Let me help you to your room."

She eased him onto the bed. He sat with his hands folded in his lap, staring at the floor, seeing nothing.

"Can I do anything for you?"

He shook his head.

"I'll leave you be, but you call me if you need anything. Have you eaten? I'll send Johnny up with sandwiches." The door closed leaving him in silence.

Minutes, hours, days later there was a knock. Johnny came in carrying a plate. "Mom said to just leave this for ya. She said something bad happened so I shouldn't bother ya. I'll come back tomorrow. Are ya gonna be okay?"

Joe hadn't moved. Johnny softly closed the door. At some point, he fell asleep. He knew this because he awoke to a soft knock.

"Mr. Clark, Mom asked me to see if ya want anything else to eat."

Joe looked at the untouched plate of sandwiches. "Not right now. Thanks."

"I'll come back later."

Joe awoke once, looked through the window. It was dark outside. Another blank in his mind, now it was light. Was it the next day or two days? Another rap sounded on the door.

"Mister Clark, telephone call for ya." Another rap. "Mister Clark?"

"Okay, Johnny. I'll be out in a second."

Every part of him ached as he looked in the mirror. His eyes were like squashed strawberries, he had stubble and the skin sagged. He splashed water on his face and staggered through the door. An immense weight hung over him, but he couldn't remember what it was. The phone lay on the table in the hall.

"Hello," he mumbled.

"Joe. It's Allison. Are you all right?"

The weight crashed down as his memory flooded back. He staggered. He was getting tired of that question. He wasn't all right, but the explanation would take time and effort he didn't have. "Yeah."

"The soldiers here the other night took all of Dawn's stuff. They said they'd deliver it to her parents. They asked me… questions. Dawn only told me you were looking into an accident that happened during the war."

"Allison, it's better if you don't know. There will be mail for her in the next few days. Put it somewhere safe. I'll get it when I get a chance. Best not to say anything to anybody. I'll tell you more when I see you."

His brain started working again. Soldiers picking up Dawn's things within hours of her accident. Who were they? How could they know about her death so quickly? How could they know about her? It had to be Dennis! Dennis said something to someone. Black hatred pushed the numbness aside. Rage engulfed him.

But wait! If they went after her, they'd come after him. He peeked out the window. No strange cars out front. But that didn't mean nobody was watching. He had to leave, but there were things to do first. Joe went to his room. He peeked out the window again at the quiet street. Silently he began packing only essentials. His rage toward Dennis shifted to those behind this.

As he sat on the bed, the headache began. At first, it was behind his eyes, but it grew stronger – spreading. The intensity increased until pain was all he felt. His vision narrowed to tiny points and winked out. The rapping on the door was thunder.

"Mr. Clark, you have another telephone call. Mr. Clark?"

"I'll be there in a minute." Joe sat up. A groan escaped his lips as his head pounded. He was nauseous and bolted past Mrs. O'Malley for the bathroom.

Mrs. O'Malley went to the phone. "Hello? Mr. Clark is indisposed at the moment."

"Yes, I'll tell him you are waiting."

She tapped on the bathroom door. "Mr. Clark, your caller said he'd wait until you could come to the phone." She heard retching. "Mr. Clark, are you sick?" Mrs. O'Malley looked at the ashen face of Joe Clark as he opened the door. She reached out to steady him. He staggered past her to the phone.

"Hello."

"Joe, it's Dennis."

"Dennis, what did you do?" he screamed.

"Joe, I can't talk long, but I had to talk to a couple of people about what you told me. They got real quiet. Listen, Buddy I may have got you in trouble. I was told to speak to no one. They were referring to you especially, but I couldn't let you hang on this. I told them I didn't know where you were living, but they can find you. Watch out. Keep your back covered. I'm sorry. This subject tromps on some big toes. I'm taking no chances, so this call is from a pay phone. Don't call me at home."

"Dennis, I think they killed Dawn." He heard a sharp intake of breath. "She was coming to see me when her car went off the road. Witnesses said it was forced off by another car. Within hours a couple hours, soldiers questioned her roommate and took Dawn's things away."

"Oh Jesus! Oh Jesus God! What have I done? Joe get out of there!"

"I'm packing my things now. After a trip to the bank, I'll disappear. Look, I'll call you at 11:30 in two days at the place we went for lunch, remember? I'll let you know what's happening."

"Joe, anything I can do, let me know. I'll talk to you Tuesday."

The pain in Joe's head subsided as he returned to his room. Passing Mrs. O'Malley he said, "Thank you. I feel better now. Mrs. O'Malley, I have to leave."

She looked at him, sadness showing on her face.

"I'm sorry to hear that, Joe, but I suspected. You had a call earlier from a man named Matt asking why you weren't at work. I told him you were sick.

"Mr. Clark, a good judge of people I am. A good man you are, God bless. Might be best if I keeps your things in the room for a while." A smile crossed her face and her eyebrows rose. "A word to Sal at the diner, and she'll tell me if you need anything."

"Is Johnny around? I'd like to say goodbye."

"I sent him on an errand. He won't take this well."

Joe nodded. "I'll leave most of my stuff. I need to travel light. You can sell it. Give the money to Johnny."

Chapter 25

Joe left through the back door. The sun wasn't up as he made his way through the deserted alleys to a bus stop. He looked around, trying to act casual. Within minutes, a bus stopped. Not caring where it went, Joe climbed on. The driver nodded at him. Joe felt as if he was in a dream. Everything was so ordinary. He changed busses several times before arriving at the main terminal. Getting his stuff from the locker, he looked at the schedule. The next bus out of town left in a few minutes going to El Paso. He took it.

Joe slept until the bus stopped in Tucson. He walked around the corner from the depot. The Congress Hotel was as he remembered on his ventures into town from Marana. Memories rose unbidden. An image of the runway appeared in his mind. His heart raced. He had to get back to the bus. Tucson was a good place, but there was too much baggage here. It was also connected. He had to keep going. Maybe one day he'd return.

Icy fingers of fear touched him. He wished he'd never contacted Dawn after getting back to the States. She'd be alive. But then he wouldn't have fallen in love with her. The ache in his heart stabbed like a dagger.

Okay, if he'd resisted telling her anything about his involvement, he'd have been working on her for that cottage with the picket fence. Joe knew he couldn't have kept it bottled up inside, especially around Dawn.

No use crying about that now. None of this could be undone. She was gone, and it was his fault. He killed another WASP. Oh, God! He wanted to dig a hole and hide, mostly from himself.

The bus pulled into Lordsburg, New Mexico. That countryside was really ugly. There was nothing but miniature bushes, sand, and rocks. He needed to stretch his legs and grab a bite. No appetite, but he had to eat something. Did the wind ever stop blowing!

In the bus depot, he read an ad on the bulletin board for help at mines in Silver City. Why not? That town was hell and gone away from anything, the perfect place to disappear.

His new bus headed down a narrow road through flat dessert toward mountains. Joe had never known miners or mines, but they used equipment. That meant maintenance. Besides, whoever heard of Silver City, New Mexico? It was as good a place to hide as any. He knew he'd have to change his name, start over as a new person. As the bus struggled up the mountains, the country got prettier. There were actually trees! It wasn't so bad.

Chapter 26

Colonel Marshall stood behind his desk, staring out his window at Washington D. C. He took a deep breath to calm himself and turned to face the two officers stiffly at attention.

"What do you mean he's disappeared?" roared the Colonel. "You had your best guys on him." He paced in front of his two subordinates. "Sit down," he commanded.

Major Rogers shrunk in his chair. "We think he had help. We were watching his rooming house, and put a tap on the phone, but he didn't come back. We checked at his workplace, and he hadn't shown up for work for several days. His boss thought he was sick.

"We searched his room. His stuff was still there. His landlady said she hadn't seen him that day. As soon as we realized he was gone, we staked out the bus and train depots. We were either too late, or he's still in Culver City."

"What about the WASP? What's going on with her?"

"She met with an unfortunate accident. Her car went off the road in a mountain pass. She was killed. We had a man on the scene collecting any information she had. They also collected everything from her room at Muroc and questioned her roommate. That loose end is tidied up," Lt Col Williams said.

"Is there any chance that this 'accident' spooked Clark?" sneered Marshall.

"It's possible," said Williams. "Perhaps we should have gone after him first, but she was the easier target. We'll keep looking. He has to turn up sometime. We're watching his rooming house and Lardner. We have people watching his foster mother's home too. He sent his paychecks there during the war. He has no place else to go. We'll find him."

"I'm sure I don't need to tell you that publicity will be bad if our little program gets out. Rogers, prepare a cover story that Clark was cracking up and started ranting like a crazy man. Out of compassion, you shipped him to a remote base so he could get away from the incident he caused. We need to be ready to discredit anything he says. There were no plugs found in the engine during our inspection. He erred in his overhaul and inspection."

"Can we alter the report to say an oil line wasn't tight? The engine lost oil pressure." asked Rogers.

"I don't want to make any more tracks, even covering up. The crash was her fault. We'll stick with the original story."

PART 2

Resurrection

R. L. Clayton

Chapter 27

November 1999

Tucson, Arizona

The woman rose from the burning ground, a flaming statue. Behind her, the broken AT-6 was upside-down, fire darkening its yellow paint. The growing cloud of thick black smoke crept toward him, blotting out the sky. Heat blistered his skin, the smell of fuel and burning flesh stung his nostrils. He had to save her. He could get no closer. She raised her arm and pointed at Joe. Her mouth opened screaming his name, her pitch rising. His own screams joined hers in macabre harmony.

Joe's eyes flew open to the dark bedroom as the echo of his own screams died. He was bathed in sweat, gasping for breath. The dream came almost nightly now, but it was different. Mary Anderson was accusing him as she died. During the Veteran's Day celebration, it always got bad, but this year was a lot worse. It had been days since he'd slept. Stiffly, he rose and shuffled into the kitchen, took a dirty glass from the cabinet and filled it with scotch. After the first deep gulp, he went to his worn recliner that fit him like a glove, fumbled with the remote and thumbed on the TV.

The screech of a woman's voice selling lawn furniture filled the room. Normally, the volume would be too loud, but here in the retirement home, everybody was asleep without their hearing aids. Only the staff would hear it. He didn't care.

Joe was going to have to do something about the dreams. With unfocused eyes, he stared at the TV until the scotch took over.

A sharp rap on the door awakened him. "Mr. Clark. You missed breakfast, and I'm checking on you to see if you're all right to make it to lunch."

Joe turned off the TV and yelled back, "Yeah, I'll be there in a few minutes." His head hurt and his stomach hadn't been good in years, but he knew if he didn't show up, they'd come for him. Lurching out of his chair, he grabbed his walker and ambled into the bathroom. The visage in the mirror was far from pretty. Patches on his face sprouted gray whiskers where he'd missed with his razor. His eyes looked like two cats going out the door.

"God! I feel like shit!"

He shed his clothes where he stood and stepped into the shower. The cold water popped his eyes open and made him flinch, but after a few seconds, he started to feel as if he'd live. The dingy towel hadn't been washed in a week, but still he used it. Good thing his housekeeper was due today. The tooth brushing was perfunctory but removed the taste of muddy feet.

He picked out a pair of tan slacks from the row of tan slacks and a plaid sports shirt in his small closet. At the messy bed, he donned them and grabbed a pair of almost clean socks from the floor. Slipping on his shoes, he headed for the door.

The hall was not empty. A stream of gray and blue-haired women pushed their walkers ahead of them like icebreakers clearing the way. Joe ducked back into his room. He tried to avoid them at all costs. They demanded conversation, and he wasn't up for that. As their leathery voices passed, he slipped out and started for the dining room. Another line of ladies started down the hall, so he turned into the library. There was only one person in there – a friend of his. They nodded at each other, acknowledging the reason for the detour.

As Joe exited the opposite door, he was in the midst of the Veterans' Day display. Flags, pictures, and mannequins wearing the uniforms of residents and contributors filled the lobby, offering a tribute to veterans. The retirement home was inhabited with veterans and wives of veterans, so they made a big deal of it. Yesterday, the commander of the local Air Force base spoke to them, and they'd all received American flags. It was a nice ceremony, one that brought tears to Joe's eyes.

When he turned away from the lobby to go into the dining room, he bumped into a small lady at one of the displays. She wore tan pants with a pink blouse. There was an emblem embroidered on it. He'd noticed her the day before. "Excuse me," apologized Joe.

"No harm," she said. "I'm just picking this up." She gestured toward the box and the carefully folded uniform.

Joe looked into her eyes. His heart skipped a beat. She reminded him of another woman, a pilot during the war, flying planes all over the country for the military. They were both pretty, with strawberry blond hair and blue eyes. Before he could stop himself, he said, "I'm Joe Clark. I was with the air maintenance group stationed out at the Marana Army Air Field during the war." Images from that time flickered in his mind. He wanted to talk to this woman. "Would you like to have lunch? The food here is pretty good, and they allow us guests."

"Thank you. I'm Sylvia James, and yes, I'd like lunch. I've eaten here before, as I know quite a few people. Someday, I'll probably move in."

At the dining room door, Joe explained he had a guest to the hostess who nodded at Sylvia. They were shown to an empty table near the window. This late in the lunch hour, there weren't many other diners. The server appeared with the menus as soon as they were seated. They looked them over.

"The chicken looks good," said Joe as he handed the menu back to the server. "Coffee for me."

"I'm going to have a large salad," said Sylvia. "Iced tea, please."

The server left and Sylvia looked at Joe. "You were at the MAAF?"

Joe chuckled. He hadn't heard that name in years. "Yes. After I got hurt at Pearl, they shipped me back to a hospital in the states and then to Marana. I spent six months before shipping out to Alaska."

He went suddenly silent as his eyes looked through Sylvia at a scene only he could see.

Sylvia watched his face change as if a cloud moved across it.

He focused on her again. "I met some WASP at the MAAF, so I know a little about them, but I'd like you to tell me more," Joe finally said.

"Well, here's the short version. When the war started, they were shipping pilots overseas as fast as they could. That created a shortage of pilots in the States. Jacqueline Cochran got an idea and spoke to

General Hap Arnold about using women as domestic pilots. They pitched it and without much of an alternative, got approval. She sent out a notification that women with pilot licenses could apply for service.

"They got a great response. The first pilots came out of training in 1943 and started ferrying planes from the factories to shipping points. We flew almost every plane in the US inventory at one time or another. WASPs did everything from test pilot to towing targets." She smiled. "All-in-all, it was quite an adventure."

"Do you still fly?"

"No. With marriage and children, there just wasn't time or money for flying."

The smile fled from Joe's face. Something broke within him, and he could no longer hold back.

"We had some of your WASPS come in to pick up planes we'd overhauled at MAAF." He closed his eyes, remembering and obviously in pain. Struggling, his voice dropped almost to a whisper, "One of them flew an AT-6 out, but it crashed, and she was killed." A moan escaped him. He blinked tears away. "The investigation said it was 'Pilot error,' but it wasn't." He shuddered and looked back up at Sylvia agony tweisting his face. "I didn't take the maintenance plugs out of the engine. I killed that girl." His hands covered his face as he moaned.

Sylvia was stunned. She watched this man, obviously in agony. It had to be an accident.

"We all made mistakes, Joe."

"It wasn't a mistake," he whispered. "I was ordered to create an incident, but it was never supposed to get anybody hurt."

Ordered! Sylvia recoiled in shock. Their food arrived, but neither picked up a fork. Sylvia's mouth remained agape as she stared at Joe. This had to be a lie, a story he was making up. Maybe he was crazy. She'd have to check this out.

He didn't look up as his shoulders shook. "I'm so sorry!" he gasped, each word coming from his soul.

Sylvia looked around the dining hall. It was deserted – they were the last ones. "Joe, when did this happen?"

In a whisper, he answered. "August 23, 1943."

"Who ordered you to leave the plugs in the engine?"

"My CO, Captain Allen Rogers. I never should have done it, but it was an order. I had to follow orders, didn't I?" He looked at her, his eyes red, tears streaking his cheeks,.

His face was pleading for agreement, that it wasn't his fault. She couldn't do that.

"Why are you telling me this?"

"The nightmares are getting worse. I can't sleep. It keeps coming back, her screams. I have to tell someone." Another sob came from him.

"You have to go to the authorities."

"With what? I have my diary and my word. The records show 'pilot error.' They'd write me off as a kook – maybe lock me up."

He was right about that. She was writing him off now.

A server approached. "We're going to be closing. Can I box those up for you?" he said, motioning toward the untouched plates. Sylvia nodded. Neither moved as the plates were cleared.

"There were more things that happened to the WASP."

This stopped Sylvia from leaving him there. "More?" she asked.

"There were other acts of sabotage committed against them. I wasn't involved, but we found out about more."

"Who's 'we?'"

"Dawn, another WASP. We found out about more."

If he was trying to get her attention, he had succeeded. She did need to find out more. She looked at him to assess if he was a danger. His head was down, his hands were in his lap. He looked… small, harmless to her. He looked beaten.

When the boxes were set on the table, they rose. Joe teetered. Instinctively, she reached out to steady him. With her arm around Joe's, she led him over to his walker.

"I want to hear more. Let's go to the library."

Chapter 28

She guided him to a corner table with two chairs. They were alone.

Tears rolled down Joe's cheeks as he slumped in the easy chair. Sylvia had never seen someone so thoroughly in despair. Incidents of sabotage were rumored, but this was the first time she'd heard about a coordinated effort. It couldn't be true! Yet before her was a man who admitted he had committed an act of sabotage and that brass was involved. If it was true, she should hate him, but he looked so pitiful.

Actually, she was worried about him. He looked like a man on the edge.

"Joe, tell me exactly what happened with those planes."

He wiped his eyes and looked at her. "We got the two AT-6s in from Sweetwater for rebuild. We knew they were being used to train WASPs. It was all over the service that you women took over the domestic flying for the military. We went through the planes completely, broke the engines down for overhaul. They'd been well cared for – they just were out of hours and due for rebuild. It took us two days to have them ready to go back in service." He nodded. "My guys were good. I did the final inspection myself."

"Joe, what is the purpose of the plugs?" She knew what the plugs were, but she wanted to hear him explain it.

"Any plane in the repair hanger has service plugs in the openings of the engine to prevent things from getting into the engine during repair work. The plugs are a standard safety procedure. These planes were scheduled to be picked up the next day. The final inspection before releasing them included pulling the plugs. That was my last check-off before for sign-out." Joe looked at his shoes.

"So you removed the plugs to take the planes through the run-up test to make sure they were ready?" This was a key question. If he had, then he had replaced them after the test run. It was no accident, but deliberate sabotage.

"Yeah, I did," he paused for a long time. "I put the service plugs back in afterward."

"When you signed out those planes, you checked off the 'Service plugs removed' box." She felt her face redden. She was ready to explode at him.

Joe stared at her, immobile and silent. He shuddered. "Yes. Yes I did," he said softly. "I only replaced the plugs in one of the planes, because an incident involving both of them would be too suspicious."

"Wouldn't the plugs be found in the investigation?" Sylvia asked. How had he or they avoided being caught?

"We were to pull the plugs after the plane ran off the runway. It was never supposed to get off the ground, just run off the end of the runway. When it did take off, it got up about a hundred feet. The engine died, and it crashed and burned." Joe's voice broke. His eyes stared at a scene only he could see. "I couldn't get to her," he cried.

Sylvia watched him closely. He took deep breath like a man rescued from drowning. Beads of sweat joined his tears as his face contorted.

"The… the fire kept us back. I blacked out. Before anybody could get to it, guards surrounded it. The Captain met with the investigation team when they came in. He must have arranged for them to pull 'em. At least there was nothing in the incident report about plugs."

"You mean you got to read the incident report?"

"Oh sure, we saw it before the inspection team left. They had the report ready the next day."

"The next day! That was quick. How long after the crash did the investigators show up?"

"The crash happened in the early morning, and the investigation team flew in that afternoon. They couldn't go out to the site right away, 'cause it was still too hot, and the fire trucks had made a mess of everything. They went out in the morning when it had cooled off and the mud had dried. They were going over that wreckage most of the day."

"When was the report completed?"

"The team met with the Captain the next day and gave him a draft. He showed it to me."

"What did the report cite as the cause of the crash?"

Joe closed his eyes. At first, Sylvia didn't think he was going to answer. He rocked back and forth. After a minute, he whispered, "Pilot error."

Fury enveloped her. Her hands shook. One of her fellow WASP had been betrayed and murdered. She was ready to wring his neck. He probably would have welcomed it.

"I went out to the site to help collect the remains." His mouth tightened into a thin line. He said no more.

"Joe, we have to do something about this!" she hissed.

He nodded mutely.

"I'll walk you back to your apartment." Joe was still nodding as she helped him stand. They left the library, her arm around him, his gait a weak shuffle. Like an old horse heading toward the barn, Joe plodded down the hall and opened his door. He looked up, as if wondering how he got there, and then moved inside. Sylvia watched Joe fall into his recliner, then entered.

She glanced around the apartment, two rooms with a kitchen and bathroom. The furnishings were obviously from his life before moving here. There was nothing fancy. There was a couch, recliner, a small table, and a TV console. With the drapes closed, a few table lamps gave a soft light to the room. The walls were bare, except for a picture of a lovely woman in uniform on his desk. It was a WASP uniform. She had strawberry blond hair, and a pretty face.

Sylvia sat on the couch across from him. "Joe, did you tell anybody else about the sabotage?" asked Sylvia, leaning forward, elbows on her knees and hands clasped tightly.

Joe stared at her with haunted eyes. "I couldn't. I'd be admitting to murder. I was going nuts. Couldn't get it out of my mind. Spending more and more time at the NCO club, drinking. My work suffered, and when an inspector caught some mistakes in an overhaul, I had to see the captain."

Sylvia's voice hardened. "This is Captain Rogers, the man who ordered you to sabotage that plane?"

"He was my CO. I told him about the nightmares. He already knew about the drinking. I told him I needed to see my priest. He seemed understanding, like he wanted to help."

Sylvia stared at him. "So they shipped you off to Ft. Glenn?"

"Sylvia, in that state, I would have killed another pilot. He was right."

"But you were still doing aircraft maintenance."

"Yeah, but I wasn't Crew Chief. Somebody was checking what I did. The change of scenery helped. I was almost able to tell myself that I had left it behind. But I didn't. The nightmare came but not as often. Ft. Glenn was a remote post, so I couldn't get booze like at Marana. Drying out helped too."

"How long were you there?"

Joe seemed to shrink into his chair. "I was there until the end of the war. I got there during the redeployment at the end of '43 and early '44 when the Aleutians were secure. It was a miserable place. Sometimes the fog was so thick you couldn't see the man in front of you. And cold! It seeped into you until it froze your bones. I've never been so cold in my life. I vowed when I got out of the service to never live anywhere cold again. That's why I'm in Arizona," stated Joe. He shivered at the memory.

Sylvia looked at her watch. "Joe, I have to know more, but it's getting late and I have errands to run. I don't like to drive after dark. Can we continue this later? It's a lot for me to think about, and my mind's not as fast as it used to be."

Joe looked at her hand on his arm. "Sure, Sylvia. Telling you about it has helped me. I might even get some sleep tonight."

Sylvia rose. "I hope so. Joe, tomorrow is pretty busy for me, but I can come back the day after. What time do you want me to come back?"

"I never get up for breakfast, so after ten would be fine."

"See you then. Now, Joe you go to dinner and get some sleep."

"'Til then." Joe raised his hand in a half wave. His mind had already drifted toward his scotch bottle in the cupboard.

Chapter 29

Joe's story had invaded Sylvia's mind. What was real truth and what was Joe's truth, she wondered. Her mind had sharpened with this story of the WASP, but now she was back in the humdrum world.

Now where did I put my keys she muttered to herself approaching the retirement home door. If my daughter got me one of those super-organizer purses like she uses, it might help. Then I'd really feel stupid when I lost them. Ah, here they are – bottom of the side pocket.

Sylvia walked through the lobby, stopping to pick up her uniform box. Joe's story was too much information that bounced from image to image. When focused on his story, her mind seemed laser sharp, but now it returned to the mundane. She wanted to get her errands done and get back home to check on a few things.

At the door, she stopped to find her dark glasses. She muttered to herself. Where did those things go? How could they get lost? One would think with glasses almost the size of my buttocks they wouldn't disappear. Aha! The super wraparounds covered half of her face. Now where did I park? Oh yes, across the street. This place needs more visitor spots. I wish I could lose some of my butt as easily as I lose my glasses.

A voice startled her. "Excuse me." The young man passed as she shuffled to one side.

Sylvia crossed the street to the sound of honking horns. She was tempted to flip them off, but ladies didn't do that. After all, she was in a crosswalk, wasn't she? She spotted her car, at least it looked like her car. Wait, her car didn't have all those dents! Maybe it did. She wasn't seeing all that well anymore.

The car was toasty warm from the sun. Ah, November in Tucson. From inside the car she couldn't see any of the dents, so that concern flew from her mind. Slowly, she backed out. A horn blew. Stomping on the brake, her hand started to rise, middle finger extended. No. no. no. She brought it back down.

Why were all these people on the road in such a hurry, she wondered. They zoomed past her. They must be doing sixty! She looked down at her speedometer. She was roaring along at a safe twenty-five, a sensible speed.

The adventure at the grocery store was normal – ten minutes looking for her list, forty-five minutes wandering the aisles asking everybody where things were, twenty minutes checking out, including the ten minutes pulling out her coupons and looking for her credit card, five more minutes looking for her keys and change to tip the boy helping her. It was exhausting.

Pulling into her carport, she heard a crunch. "Oh, damn!" Sylvia swore aloud. She'd hit the parking bumper again. Oh well. Okay, the dents <u>were</u> hers. The house had been home for almost forty years. After seeing Joe's apartment, her home was spacious. When her whole family lived here it seemed small, but now it was only her. Well, also

Harold's ashes there on the bookshelf. God she missed that man.

Half the house was closed off, so she didn't have to heat and air condition it. Her closets and cupboards were full of the things of her life. To anybody else, it would seem a horrendous mess, but everything had its place, and she knew where everything was.

After putting her uniform carefully away, she got a tall glass of iced tea and a small glass of Southern Comfort. Pulling out her WASP book, a jar of peanut butter, and a box of crackers, she sat in her easy chair. With her magnifying glass in hand, she began to read.

The crick in her neck told her she'd been at this too long. Sylvia looked at her watch. After midnight! She must have dozed off. The folded napkin served as a bookmark as she closed the book.

There had been a crash in Marana. It was in the book.

Joe was right.

Rising to the tune of creaking and cracking joints, she steadied herself before tottering toward the bedroom. Her mind swirled with the events of the day. Too tired, she thought. Without undressing, she fell into her bed and was asleep in minutes.

Chapter 30

Sylvia tried to open her eyes – they were glued shut. It took three tries to sit up. Looking down, she was astonished to find herself fully dressed. I must have been really tired last night, she muttered.

In the shower, she held onto the grab bar like a puppy with a throw toy. The stinging water revived her. In her bathrobe, she fixed her oatmeal and coffee, retrieved the WASP book from her chair, and sat at the table.

The book opened at the marked page and she resumed her search.

There it was:

Mary Anderson. August 23, 1943. AT-6 Crashed upon takeoff, at Marana Army Air Field. Aircraft a total loss, pilot killed. Cause: Pilot Error.

The confirmation stunned her. It had seemed like a story until she read this.

The clock showed nine-o'clock. She needed to get ready to go to her P. E. O. (Philanthropic Educational Organization) meeting, and then the church board meeting. A day full of meetings that now seemed trivial.

From her closet, she pulled out tan pants and a blouse with light orange flowers. Anklets and her sneakers finished her ensemble. A brush through her hair a few times took care of her do, a swipe with her favorite lipstick and she stepped back. Not great, but good enough. Time to go.

At the meetings, Sylvia's mind refused to focus on the business. The P. E. O.
lunch was the normal cardboard chicken with lumpy gravy. The dessert was chocolate cake, and she finished hers quickly.

"Would you like mine?" the woman on her right asked. Sylvia restrained herself from snatching it. Tomorrow, I'll start my diet, she ordered herself, taking the offered plate.

The church board meeting droned on as Pastor Tim explained why the library couldn't buy more books. They have to make an appeal. Attendance had been falling as parishioners continued to die off. Young people just didn't attend church anymore.

What they needed was a bake sale. Sylvia offered the suggestion to a lukewarm reception. People didn't eat sweets now either. That new-normal attitude had bypassed Sylvia.

It was late afternoon by the time she arrived at home. Crash! Got the parking bumper again. She really did need a smaller car. But would she feel safe in one of those little things? Her Caprice was a boat that floated safely down the road.

Entering the kitchen, she put her purse and keys on the counter. In the den, her WASP book beckoned. She needed to talk to someone else about Joe's story. She called, Maryanne, a sister WASP who knew everything.

The phone rang "I am sorry, but you have reached a number that is not in service or has…" She slammed the receiver down. Why didn't they make these phones with readable numbers? On the third try she got an answer. "Hello, Maryanne, it's Sylvia James."

"Sylvia, I haven't talked to you in weeks. How are you?"

"Oh, I'm fine. How are you?"

"I've had this urinary tract infection, and it's getting bad."

"Have you seen the doctor?"

"I'm going in tomorrow."

"The reason I called is yesterday I had a strange experience, and I can't get it out of my head. It's about a crash in Marana in 1943 where a WASP was killed." Sylvia related Joe's story.

"Sylvia, that wasn't the only incident," said Maryanne. "In 1944, I had a near-crash in Texas when my engine stalled on takeoff. Luckily, I had enough altitude to bring it around and land.

"There was sugar in the gas tank, but the report was 'pilot error'. I wrote the incident up in my log book, for all the good that did. There were other incidents like that, but all official records show 'pilot error'. What do you want to do about this? It's old history."

"Joe thought there were more people involved, some of them brass. I'm not sure. Maybe it's time these stories came out. I knew of a few instances myself, but I thought they were random. Joe's story suggests a conspiracy that included higher ups."

"Sylvia, if you want to research it, contact Dr. Phyllis Peterson at the Texas Women's University. She's watching over the repository of WASP history. She can assist you. I'll help where I can."

"I'll talk to Joe tomorrow to see what he wants to do. As a witness, he's key to bringing this out."

"Sylvia, I was mad about the sugar in my gas tank, but I got over it. By now, those involved are probably dead or near dead. The world has moved on."

"Yeah you're right, but I see Joe, whose life was ruined, Mary, who's dead, and I want someone to acknowledge they were wrong. Can I get your logbook and the incident report from you?"

"Sure. Go ahead and investigate. Keep me informed, but there's too much chocolate in the world for me to waste my time on that."

They both laughed.

Chapter 31

Sylvia lived close to Joe's retirement home. The drive was short and traffic light this time of day. There was even a parking place in the visitor's lot. As she pulled into the space, her bumper clipped the sign. "Damn." Another dent.

With her WASP books in a bag hanging from her arm, she shuffled from the car to the entrance. The door opened automatically. In the doorway, she stopped to remove her dark glasses, fumbling them into her purse.

"Excuse me. Could I get by?" A young woman in a brown UPS uniform squeezed around her.

"I'm sorry," Sylvia mumbled.

Thanksgiving decorating was underway in the lobby. Inflatable pumpkins lined the walls, and cornucopias were on the tables. Incense smelling like autumn leaves burning lent atmosphere. Several people sat in the chairs and couches. The gas fireplace added to the homey air in the room. Joe was not in the lobby, so she went down the hall to his door. She knocked loudly.

"Come in."

She stepped through his doorway. The curtains were drawn, the room lit by the glow from the TV. There was no sound. Joe was in his recliner "Hi, Joe. How are you today?"

Joe was in his bathrobe with tattered slippers on his feet. "Do you know how to turn on the sound? I can't get this damn thing to work." He held up the remote.

She took it and pointed it toward the TV, pushing the mute button. Sound blasted out. In the dim light, she searched to find the volume button. Failing that, she pushed the red power button. The silence was abrupt.

"Joe, are you okay?"

"Eh?"

Dragging out each word she said, "ARE-YOU-OKAY?"

His eyebrows rose. "Isn't it a little early for wine? I don't like Tokay myself, so I never buy it. I do have scotch. You want that instead?"

Shaking her head, Sylvia pointed at her own hearing aids.

"Eh? Yah, okay. Let me get them." He heaved himself up and disappeared into the bedroom. A few minutes later, he appeared fumbling with his ears. "Sorry, I'm usually by myself, so I don't put these in until lunch."

Sylvia focused, pushing aside the fog of her daily life as she sat on the couch. She felt her mind sharpening. "Joe, I found a listing of the incident in my WASP book. You were right. Mary Anderson was killed on takeoff in an AT 6." Sylvia watched Joe withdraw as the memory surfaced. Head bowed, his shoulders shook.

In a soft voice, Sylvia said, "I want to hear more about what happened. Who's the WASP in the picture?" she said, pointing at the black and white photo on his desk.

Joe looked at the photo then back at Sylvia. They could be sisters, he thought. "That's Dawn

Dunham. She was the other pilot on that day. I met her and Mary the night before at dinner."

"Oh," said Sylvia, looking at the picture. "Pretty girl." She waited for Joe to say more. The silence grew.

Joe's gaze was glued to the photo. He wiped his eyes. "I wrote letters to her every week from Alaska. She was so busy sometimes they didn't catch up to her for a month. When she did write, they were short letters. She had to write family too. At times, her letters were only a sentence or two. Stuff like, 'I'm in New York picking up a P-51 to take to Canada. It's cold here, but probably not as cold as where you are.'

"We never mentioned anything about the crash when we wrote. I hadn't told her about the plugs, but I thought she blamed me because I was the mechanic.

"She never said anything about beaus. With all that travel, she wouldn't have a chance to see anybody. She never mentioned it anyway."

"What do you mean? Joe," asked Sylvia.

Joe turned away, saying nothing for a while. "I guess I hoped she thought of me as someone she'd like to know. Anyway, I started writing a diary while I was at Fort Glenn. There wasn't much else to do. Even Dawn never knew about it. A lot of pain lives in those pages." He pointed to a small worn book next to the photo of Dawn. "I've come close to burning it more than once. Maybe it'll see the light of day sometime." Joe sighed from deep in his soul.

Chapter 32

"Did you see Dawn again?" asked Sylvia.

Joe nodded. "She told me about a job she had when the WASP were disbanded. Ya know, that was another rotten deal for the WASP. With a flowery speech, they were told they weren't needed and to go home. No bus fare, no train fare.

"After seeing the world from the hottest planes in the world, Dawn wasn't ready to settle down in her small home town. A bay mate told her about some secret job as a mechanic on some new type of airplane, so she went to California.

"I went to visit when I got back to the States." Joe was silent. "We got together. I had visions of marrying her, having a couple of kids, the house with the white picket fence, the whole American dream. I knew I had to tell her about the real reason for the crash that killed her friend, but I was scared she'd hate me." Joe shook his head. "I never should have gone to see her."

"What happened when you told her?" asked Sylvia.

"She hated me." Joe looked at the floor. He was silent for almost a minute. "But she couldn't let it end with me.

"I went back to Pasadena, got a job, lived okay. I kept writing, trying to apologize. I never got a letter back. I tried calling, but she wouldn't talk to me. If only she'd left it like that."

"You did hear from her, didn't you?"

He nodded slowly. "She showed up at my rooming house one day. She was mad as hell and wanted me to help her find out who was behind this program of sabotage. If only I'd said no, she might have dropped it, but I wanted to be with her again. I thought this was a path back to her." He looked up, pleading for understanding.

"You did help her. What happened?"

"Oh yeah, I helped her," he sneered. "I went back to Washington D. C. and went through records, looking for Captain Rogers and whoever was in on it with him. I got names, but in the process I got my childhood friend who helped me in trouble. Then I got Dawn killed." He broke down, his face in his hands sobbing. "It's all in the diary. Take it." He waved one hand toward the desk.

Sylvia looked at the wreck of a man in front of her. Her heart went out to his tormented soul.

A knock on the door startled them. "Mr. Clark, you need to go to lunch. There's only a few minutes before the dining room closes."

Joe looked at Sylvia as he shouted, "Yah, okay I'll be there in a couple of minutes." He shrugged. "I missed breakfast, so they send the nanny to get me for lunch." He reached for his scotch glass. It was empty. He gazed at it.

Sylvia rose. "Joe, pull yourself together and get cleaned up. I'll wait for you in the dining room. We'll go to lunch together."

Joe sniffed at his soiled bathrobe, sniffed again, wrinkled his nose. He looked at his tattered slippers. "Good idea." He struggled up from his chair and headed for the bathroom.

Closing the door, she leaned against the wall. Did she really want to do this? Opening up this sordid history required Joe, but he was a major project all by himself. She needed to read his diary, learn more about him. In a way, he reminded her of her husband, Harold, but weaker.

In the dining room, Sylvia talked about herself, staying away from talk of the past. It wasn't the time or place. Joe needed a break from this story.

"I have a daughter living here in Tucson, and a granddaughter going to school in Flagstaff. My daughter wants me to move in here, but I'm not ready. Since Harold died, it's been difficult. We never planned on living apart, but I've been in the same house for forty years. It's full of the things of our life.

"Taking care of my house is a chore, but I don't know what I'd do with my time without it. My church and service groups help to keep me busy. And keep the loneliness away. My daughter calls a couple of times every week to check up on me, and we go to lunch a once or twice a month. I get to see my granddaughter, Erica, on holidays. She likes to stay with me." Sylvia realized she was prattling on.

"How long since your husband died?" asked Joe, the first time he'd spoken.

"It's been five years. At first it was really hard, but I keep on from day to day. It's all we can do."

Joe grunted.

Sylvia made a snap decision. "Would you like to come over for Thanksgiving dinner? It'll be better than what's served here, if only because of the company." She laughed a little nervously.

"If you're sure it would be okay. I mean, I don't want to intrude on your family."

"It's my house. I get to invite whoever I want." She laughed.

Joe laughed too, but his laughter descended into racking cough. He recovered. "Yeah, I'd like that, I'd like that a lot."

"You don't sound good."

His face was red from coughing, There were beads of sweat on his forehead.

"Yeah, I've been feeling a little punk lately. Haven't got much energy, and this cough sprang up yesterday."

"You should go the doctor and get checked out."

"Nah, I'll be okay. I know what's good for me." Joe smiled.

It looked more like a grimace to Sylvia. It's the same thing her husband would have said.

Back at his apartment, Sylvia said, "Joe I have a few things to do today, but I'd like to take your diary with me. I'll come back in a couple of days. Would that be all right?"

Joe frowned. The past had come back. "Yeah, sure. Take it. You can keep it if you want."

He coughed again.

"Joe, get that cough checked out. At least go see the nurse here."

"Yeah maybe I will." He fell into his chair. He knew he wouldn't.

Chapter 33

Sylvia rubbed her neck. The crick hadn't gone away for a while. She'd been reading Joe's diary since she got home from the retirement home. It was past midnight now. Not a diary in the normal sense of day-to-day entries, it held a full accounting starting with the orders from Captain Rogers to sabotage the AT-6 and the crash. A tormented soul poured out events and anguish.

His tour in Alaska was a blessing and a curse. It was a blessing because the site of the crime was physically remote, allowing him to isolate himself from it. But Alaska was a curse because there was little to do but work. Joe poured out his heart in these pages. He spoke of his love for Dawn, how each letter he received, no matter how brief, became a ray of sunshine in the darkness of that hellhole. It was hell, and he deserved that and much worse.

He told of his return to the States, going to Muroc to see Dawn, and how he was driven to admit his complicity, yet torn about how it would effect her. His honesty with himself was rare, Sylvia thought. In Joe's mind, he killed Mary because he was weak, and the guilt was a huge burden.

Dawn's total rejection of Joe left him numb, an unthinking creature only surviving. Again, he felt he deserved the punishment. He'd jumped at the chance to redeem himself in her eyes, but more so in his own.

Joe told of being in an impossible position when he went to Washington D. C. He betrayed his lifelong friend, jeopardizing everything Dennis spent his lifetime building for his family, yet he knew he had to have the information to right the wrong done years before. It represented another brick of guilt heaped on the towering pile.

The murder of Dawn nearly broke him. After the panicked flight from California, he reached the pit of despair, mechanically going through survival. As time passed, his entries became less introspective. He spoke of the gritty work in the mines, occasionally hearing of some unfortunate who died in an accident. The dangers of mine work were acceptable risks. At last, he became too old to do his job. His return to Tucson was inevitable.

Joe's dairy was dark and black. Sylvia never came across a passage of happiness. He spoke of someday finishing what Dawn started, exposing those behind the sabotage, seeking redemption.

Sylvia decided to help Joe, not because she felt sorry for him (she did), but because it was the right thing to do. Her sisters were murdered, others attacked. Yes, it was an attack. Those responsible got away with it. But not forever, if she had anything to do about it.

As she prepared for bed, Sylvia formed a plan. First they had to find out information about Allen Rogers, Jake Williams, and the others Joe found during his search more than fifty years ago. Sleep did not come easily. With the internet, Erica, her computer whiz granddaughter, could help. After they knew more, they'd formulate a strategy to expose what had been done.

Sylvia rose later than usual after her late night. The coffee revived her. The glance at her WASP book triggered an idea. Dawn should be in there.

She looked up the name Dawn Dunham. Here she was:

Class of 43-3. Deceased 1946.

Again the reality of Joe's tale struck her. She had yet to find anything untrue. Joe's diary spoke to his hope of marrying Dawn, settling down and having kids. It also spoke of the agony her death brought to him. She needed to see Joe again, explain what she wanted to do. She'd have to be careful. He was more fragile than he appeared.

Now that she decided to pursue this, she needed Joe. He was the key in exposing these crimes.

Her breakfast was the usual oatmeal and protein drink. As she dressed, she marveled at how alive she felt with this new purpose in her life. She didn't hit the parking bumper as she pulled out to go to the retirement home.

Chapter 34

Sylvia's knock on Joe's door was answered by a shouted "Come in" followed by coughing. His curtains were drawn, the apartment dark, lit only by the television set. Joe was in his recliner dressed in the same clothes as yesterday.

"Joe, we must talk more, but first you need to clean up," she said in a tone she used as a mother. "Meet me in the lobby when you've showered and dressed." It was not a request Joe could refuse.

"Yeah, okay. You're right. I need to get moving. If I don't go to lunch, the Gestapo nanny will drag me there. It's embarrassing." With a groan, he heaved himself up. As he tottered toward the bathroom, Sylvia left.

Twenty minutes later, a freshened-up Joe approached her in the lobby.

"You look a lot better," she said.

"I feel a lot better. Thanks for kicking my butt into gear. Let's go get in line for lunch. I'm hungry."

Sylvia again opted for the salad bar. Joe ordered a tuna sandwich. She looked around the dining room. The ratio of women to men was better than four to one. "Why do those women keep staring at us?" asked Sylvia, nodding toward an adjacent table.

"You've noticed there aren't many men here. They want to know who you are poaching on their territory." Joe laughed. "I've never been the object of female attention before. I don't like it. They always want to talk. It takes too much energy and gets on my nerves."

They ate in silence.

Walking back to Joe's apartment, she noticed his pace was slower, more labored. He plopped into his recliner. Sylvia opened the curtains, flooding the room with light. She settled on the couch.

"Joe, did you go to the nurse?"

He shook his head. "Naw, I wanted to give myself a chance to get better."

"You're not better, though, are you?"

"Well, maybe."

"Am I going to have to walk you there?" She shook her finger at him.

Joe smiled at the gesture. "I'll go today. I promise."

"I read your diary. It affected me, and I want to help you get these criminals. I'm going to get my granddaughter to help search for Allen Rogers and Jake Williams. We'll look for some of the other names from your Washington trip. With that information, we'll figure out what to do."

Joe nodded. "I couldn't do it by myself."

No kidding, Sylvia thought.

"You went to Washington. Tell me about Dennis."

Joe sighed as his mind focused. "In high school, Dennis and I were best pals. During our senior year, he saw lot of Jacqui. They were high school sweethearts. The wedding was rushed with Jacqui showing a little. Billy arrived six months later, a real cutie. Of course, they both were expelled from school." Joe shook his head, frowning.

Sylvia nodded. It was a different time with different rules.

Joe cleared his throat. "We drifted apart with his new life as a family man, living with her parents. Dennis was taking classes at night to get his high school diploma while working at the Five and Dime. It was a tough life. Then the war broke out. We joined up together. The Army, in its wisdom, put him into clerk school and me into mechanic school. At least they got that right. Army life pulled us apart."

Sylvia gave him a sad smile. "I know how that happens. Once we started flying, it would be weeks before mail would catch up to us. I didn't see friends for months."

Joe coughed and ran his hand through his thin hair. "We didn't write much. Most of his letters went to his wife, of course. I remember his note about married life and being a father, but he sent that while I was in Alaska. I was so blue, nothing mattered."

Their eyes met. "I haven't spoken to Dennis since that last phone call. We knew they'd be watching him to find me. I felt terrible for pulling him into this mess, but Dawn and I didn't know what else to do." Joe's eyes drifted away from her. "That's not an excuse, is it? I also put some of the blame for Dawn's murder on him. It was me that set the whole thing in motion though. I found it easy not to talk to him after what I did. I thought about him, but felt guilty, so I pushed him aside."

Sylvia wondered, what happened to Dennis. Erica could search, but if it turned out to be bad news, it would be best not to tell Joe. More guilt would weaken him, and she needed him strong. She had to find out everything she could about him. He had weaknesses, but he was strong on ethics and loyalty.

"You didn't write a lot about your life in Silver City. How long were you there?"

"Until I retired from the mines, forty years. Then I moved in here and changed my name from Dunham back to Clark."

"Dunham! You took Dawn's last name?"

"I couldn't think of much but her, and no one would be the wiser. Nobody figured it out." Joe shrugged. "At that point, I almost didn't care."

"What was life like there?"

"The climate was a lot cooler than California or Arizona, and a lot better than Alaska. In many ways, it was like the old west mining camps, with lots of men, bars, and bawdy houses. Saturday nights at the Buckhorn Saloon and Opera House got wild at times, but not for me. I still carried a torch for Dawn, so my social life was pretty dull. There was always someone ready to take your money.

"Mechanic and maintenance work is different for the mines. Everything is heavy duty. Unlike aircraft work, weight means nothing. Everything has to be sturdy. Those guys can break a steel block." Joe grinned. "The other thing was that small mistakes rarely resulted in somebody dying." He looked at her. "That was important to me. I couldn't take another death on my conscience."

Joe smiled, remembering his work in maintenance for the mines. "It was a good job. The people were decent though a little rough at times. It was dangerous work. We'd lose a couple of guys every year. Mainly, I kept my head down and did my job." Joe looked at the photo on his desk. "I still love

Dawn, the memories haven't faded, but the pain lessened in Silver City. When I was too old to do the work, I came back. So here I am." He shrugged.

"But the dreams have come back, haven't they?" stated Sylvia.

A flash of pain crossed Joe's face. He took a deep breath and looked out the window. "With no work to occupy my mind, Dawn and Mary haunt me."

"Joe, we have to face this and bring it out. You can't keep on like this." Sylvia watched his lips thin as he looked into her eyes and nodded. "My granddaughter, Erica, is coming home for Thanksgiving. She can help in our search for Major Rogers, Colonel Marshall, and Colonel Williams. She's a whiz at the computer."

Chapter 35

Joe liked Sylvia's house. It was an older ranch style home, roomy with wide eaves and lots of windows to let in light. Their family group was small. Erica Chambers, Sylvia's granddaughter was a bubbly dark haired twenty-something college student. Sylvia's daughter, Sharon Chambers, was pretty, a slender strawberry blond, and helped Sylvia in the kitchen. Her ex, Erica's father, was not invited.

"Sylvia, what a great feast. You were so kind to ask me to be part of your family today."

"You are very welcome. After dessert, Erica and I have a surprise for you."

Joe blanched and put his hand to his heart. "A little indigestion," he explained. "It happens when I eat too much."

"We found them!" blurted out the bubbly teen. Joe could see a lot of Sylvia in her, the same curly blond hair and ski slope nose.

After coffee, they went into Sylvia's office and gathered around Erica seated at the computer.

"Colonel Williams was deceased, seven years ago." On the screen was a photo of an Army officer in uniform with full award display on his chest. Listed in his service record was his time as Special Training Officer, 389th Army Air Force Base Unit, AAF West Coast Training Center. He retired in 1982 and died in 1992, survived by a wife and two children.

"Here's Brigadier General Ted Marshall," said Erica. Another uniformed Army officer appeared with medal regalia on his chest. "He retired from service in 1975 and died in 1990."

"Major Rogers is still alive and living in Virginia," pointed out Sylvia.

Joe raised his eyebrows. "Rogers is in Virginia?" A tremor ran through him, a mixture of fear and hatred. The man who ruined his life was no longer a phantom.

"Erica's done some sleuthing. After retiring from the Army, he went into politics. His family had money and ties, and Marshall and Williams were on his political team. He spent twenty-three years as the Senator from Virginia before retiring." Sylvia was shocked when she learned of Rogers. With concern, she watched for Joe's reaction.

Joe's mouth hung open, his face reddened. "Senator!" he roared. "He kills people and becomes a senator! What happened to this country?" A coughing fit bent him over.

"Take it easy, Joe. Here, sit down." Sylvia helped him into the chair Erica vacated. Joe's breathing steadied. "We're going to get him." Her flinty eyes sparkled. "He's living in a gated community called Lake of the Woods in Locust Grove near Fredericksburg. I think we should consider a visit. Do you want me to book two tickets? Because I'm going." Sylvia put her hands on her hips.

Joe slumped. "And do what?" he sighed. "You think I haven't thought about this. I had plans. I dreamed of facing him, then what? Even given a weapon, I couldn't kill him. It's just not in me. But I do want him to pay," Joe coughed

Sylvia tightened her jaw. "The one thing we go after is his reputation. The public will know he is a murderer. So you're going with me?" She looked down at him.

"I am. I want to confront him. We're in this together." He looked up at her.

"Are you okay?" she asked, worry evident in her voice.

Something was wrong. Beads of sweat dotted his forehead, his face was gray, his chest heaved as he gasped. "I'm not breathing so good. My chest hurts."

"I'm calling 911." Sylvia cried and grabbed the phone.

Joe tried to raise a hand to stop her but couldn't.

Sylvia and her family watched the EMTs roll Joe out to the ambulance. "I'm going to the hospital," said Sylvia. "Can you take care of things here?"

Erica nodded.

The ten-minute drive to the hospital seemed to last hours as Sylvia's mind raced. Was the news too much? Was Joe going to be all right? She parked and walked in.

"I'm looking for Joe Clark. He was just brought in," she said to the receptionist who typed on her computer.

"He's in emergency. He's going in for testing and evaluation shortly."

"Can I see him?"

"Only for a few minutes. He's in space 211."

Sylvia went through the automatic doors, asking a nurse where 211 was. She pointed to the numbers painted on the wall. Sylvia followed the hall until she found Joe in his bed under the number 211. His eyes fluttered open as she neared. His mouth moved, but the words were too soft. She leaned close.

"Don't go without me," he whispered. His eyes closed, and an aide wheeled the bed into the bowels of the hospital.

Chapter 36

Sylvia walked down the tiled hall at the rehab center. Aids in green scrubs moved patients in wheelchairs in and out of rooms. The exercise room had people passing large rubber balls around and exercising with elastic bands. She knocked on the open door of room twenty-two.

"Joe, how are you today?" asked Sylvia. She'd been visiting Joe every day since his heart attack and surgery. Physically, he was recovering, but his mood had been low. She was concerned for him.

Joe stared out the window in silence.

"Your doctor tells me you're going to be leaving rehab tomorrow."

"Yeah, my coverage ran out. I'm not well enough to go back to independent living at the retirement home. They're moving me to a nursing home until an assisted care apartment opens up. I can't tell you how happy that makes me."

"Oh, Joe, I'm so sorry."

"Sylvia, don't worry about it. It's what life is at our age. But I don't have to like it."

Desperately Sylvia sought a way of cheering him up. "I want to wish you a Merry Christmas."

"Bah," exclaimed Joe in his best Scrooge voice. "I've been visited by the ghost of Christmas Past, and I'm not looking forward to Christmas Present in the nursing home. They won't let me drink scotch."

Sylvia looked Joe in the eye. "Joe, you've got to improve, and it's a slow process. I've made our flight reservations to Virginia for late spring. I have some other news.

"Senator Allen Rogers resigned for health reasons. He had a heart attack in October. According to the news releases, he's expected to recover but decided to step down. The governor has appointed a new senator to finish out his term. Rogers is recuperating at home.

"You have to get well. You've lost weight since your surgery. Start eating so we can go face Rogers."

"Have you tasted the food in here?" He pointed to the tray on his table.

Sylvia had to admit that the half-eaten hot dog didn't look very appetizing. Even the chocolate pudding looked lumpy. Maybe it was tapioca.

"Everybody loses weight here. It's their diet plan," exclaimed Joe. "Never thought I'd say I miss the retirement home food, but I do. It is gourmet compared to this."

"Joe, are you up to Christmas with my family? There'll be eggnog, the adult homemade version. Santa might bring you a present."

Joe's eyes brightened. "I've been a good boy. Maybe some scotch – good scotch?"

Sylvia laughed. "Perhaps. I'll come get you some after you get moved in."

True to her word, Sylvia picked Joe up on Christmas Eve. The drive to her house was very short. The house smelled wonderful as they entered.

"We're here," called Sylvia.

"Just in time. Everything's on the table," said a voice from the kitchen.

"Grandma, the ham was delicious," said Erica.

"I hope you saved room for dessert." Sylvia smiled. "I made two kinds of pie, mince and pumpkin. You can have either or both.

"Joe, how are you doing?"

"Sylvia, thank you for inviting me to be with you and your family again. You've made what promised to be a bleak holiday into a nice time."

"What'll it be for dessert?" asked Erica, removing Joe's plate.

"Mince has always been my favorite. Don't see it so much anymore," Joe answered.

"One mince pie coming up, Mister Clark."

"Grandma, what do you want?"

"I'll take a little of both, please. Thanks for helping."

Sylvia's Christmas tree was amazing. It was so laden with ornaments that the branches were barely visible. The collection of ornaments represented decades of past Christmases. Joe leaned heavily on his cane as he walked around the tree looking at the amazing array. He was still a little unsteady, but he'd left his wheelchair at the rehab center home. It was a pain to tote around.

Finally, the clatter in the kitchen quieted.

"Gift time," said Sylvia.

Erica was in charge of distributing the packages. Gifts of sweaters, socks, and makeup brought smiles to their faces. Joe was surprised when Erica handed him a shoebox-sized package. He looked up to see Sylvia's grin. Joe began to unwrap it carefully.

Erica laughed. "Joe, we don't save wrapping paper. Let'er rip."

Inside the box was a model of a 1959 Corvette. It was heavy. Joe looked up, smiling.

"It's part of the Beam Collection," said Sylvia. She took it from him, opening the trunk. Inside was a bottle top. "Originally, it had Jim Beam in it, but we drank that, so I filled it with scotch. You might be able to get away with keeping this in your room."

Joe started laughing and couldn't stop. This was a Christmas present!

Chapter 37

Sylvia wrinkled her nose at the smell in the hallway of the nursing home. People were sitting in wheelchairs in various states of consciousness. No aides were to be seen.

She knocked on Joe's door.

Joe turned in his wheelchair to look from the TV to her. "Come in." He smiled happily.

"Hey, Joe, thought I'd stop in to see how life is here." She glanced at Joe's roommate. He hadn't moved since her knock, his eyes glued to the TV, his mouth slack. The room reeked of soiled linens.

A wry smile crossed Joe's grizzled face. "Oh, life here is grand. Burt over there hasn't stirred, and nobody answers the ring to come change him. I'm fortunate I can at least go to the bathroom on my own."

"How's the therapy going?" asked Sylvia.

"It's going well. I'm only sitting in this wheelchair because it's more comfortable than any of the chairs. I've gotten some energy back. They may let me out early for good behavior."

"Have you arranged to move back to the retirement home?"

"We're arguing over whether I can go back to independent living or into assisted living. I'm holding out for my old apartment." Joe's eyes twinkled

"That's great news. I came over to share a little New Years Eve cheer with you. Where's your car? I'll put some medicine in it." Sylvia looked around the room.

"Some asshole stole it," Joe growled.

"Did you report it?" asked Sylvia, her voice hardening.

"Of course, but nothing came of it. Stuff disappears all the time here. It's worse than a New Delhi train station."

"Joe, I'll be back in a few minutes."

Sylvia fumed. That car was part of a collection. At the nurse's station she asked for the supervisor. She waited while the nurse called, her anger obvious by her crossed arms and tapping foot. She had grown quite protective of Joe,

The obese man with black framed glasses walked up and introduced himself. "I'm Mr. Brody. How may I help you?"

"I'm Sylvia James, and my friend, Joe Clark, reported a missing car model to you a day ago. Have you recovered it?"

"I haven't heard about that. When did this item get misplaced?"

"Within the last week. If you can't get that back within one hour, I'm going to call the Sheriff's Department and report a theft. They will start an investigation, something I'm sure you wouldn't care for."

"What did this toy look like?"

"It's not a toy. It's part of the Jim Beam collection, a model of a red 1959 Corvette. It is valuable."

"These things take time. I'll start asking," he stammered.

"You have one hour before I dial 911."

"Please, Mrs. James. It will take more time to check this out."

"Mr. Brody, one hour. After that, I file the report. Then I'm contacting my attorney about a lawsuit." She spun away from him, heading back to Joe's room. She noted the blinking call light above the door.

"Joe, I don't know if I did any good getting your gift back, but I do have some 'medicine' here. How about a scotch? Where's ice?"

Joe pointed at the water pitcher on the tray.

"To our investigation," said Sylvia, holding her paper cup out to Joe. They touched cups.

"How's that going?" asked Joe.

"I'm just getting started with your files. In addition to your diary and your account, I'm also going back to the WASP to get photocopies of the incident logs. The Texas Women's University is helpful. Many of the WASP gave their logbooks along with photos and uniforms and... and everything. I want to compile a report with the official incident report and the logbook entry."

Joe brightened at the news of progress. Sylvia liked the smile on his face.

There was a knock at the door. An aide stood with Joe's car in his hands. "I understand this is yours," he said, handing it to Joe. "We were holding it for safe keeping."

"Thank you," Joe said. "Can you check on my roommate? He hasn't moved all day."

Sylvia and Joe watched as the aide checked the still form. He drew the sheet over his face and left.

Joe sighed, shaking his head. "Well, Burt didn't make it until the millennium. Let's have another scotch." Joe hoisted his car. "The celebration here starts at 4:00 because nobody, including staff, will be awake at midnight. So," he held out his cup, "here's to a successful 2000." In his mind, Joe could see an end to his torment. But before that was the huge obstacle of facing Rogers.

Chapter 38

Sylvia looked at the purple bunting and pink heart-shaped balloons in the dining room at the retirement home. Tired-gay was how she'd describe it. Her lavender pants and light rose blouse fit right in. People were working too hard at being festive.

"Joe, thanks for inviting me over for Valentine's Day lunch." Reaching into her purse, she took out a small bag and handed it to him. "Happy Valentine's Day."

He took out a pink frosted cookie. "Thank you, I got you something too." He handed her a small box. "Local artisans set up tables in the lobby a few days ago. This made me think of you."

Sylvia moved her salad plate to one side, making space for the box. Inside was a small model of a P-51. A wide smile covered her face.

"Joe, this is great. It was my favorite plane to fly."

"I think it was the favorite of every pilot who flew it." Joe grinned.

"Let's go back to your room. I want to bring you up to date on the investigation."

She watched Joe in his tan slacks and checked shirt walk down the hall ahead of her. "You're moving pretty well. How are you feeling?"

Opening the door, he smiled. "Almost as good as before the heart attack. I'm keeping up with the exercises and watching what I eat. I still like my steak, but they don't serve it here. We can go out. I'll buy."

"You're on." Sylvia wrinkled her nose as she entered. In the dim light, she saw a pile of dirty laundry.

"Let's open a window in here." She drew the curtains and opened the sliding glass door. "How would you feel about a trip back east after Easter?"

"Yeah, I'm up for that." Joe sat in his recliner. "Let me know the schedule and what it costs. I'll get you a check."

Sylvia sat on the couch. She had been worried that Joe might not be able to make the trip, but he looked eager to go.

"My granddaughter, Erica, can get us tickets. She's been checking the internet for more information on Allen Rogers, too. We haven't found any death announcement. I'm sure there would be one." She watched Joe's jaw clench.

"What kept me going during my time in the hospital, rehab, and the nursing home was the thought that someday I'd face him. Confront him with what he did. Where are you with the incident reports and log books?"

"Erica downloaded the reports and copies of the logbooks from the archives. Maryanne – she was in the class before me – and I have been matching them up, putting together a report. We should have everything done before Easter."

He nodded. It was coming together. "Make copies." Joe wanted copies for any eventuality.

"Erica found a lot of information on Allen Rogers as a senator. He brought government contracts to the state, a lot of jobs. His social services record isn't as good, and in the elections, his opponents attacked him on that, but he had the money. After his heart attack, the governor appointed his own crony to fulfill the term. Now, Roger's son, Jeff, is running for the senate seat."

"Keeping power in the family," muttered Joe.

Sylvia shook her head. "Erica also looked into Jeff's record. He's cut from different cloth than his father. He's been a public defender, representing minority business in opposing his father's machine. He married a Hispanic woman, only his mother came to the wedding. The rumor is he and his father aren't on best terms, but Rogers is backing his election campaign."

"Interesting." Joe looked out the window for a moment. "After we confront Rogers, what's next?"

"Maryanne has contacts in Washington who can get us a news interview. After that, we'll hold a news conference."

Joe nodded. It was a good plan. "No contact with the Army before. I'm afraid they'd try to bury it,"

"There is no advantage for us to contact them first. We can meet with them to turn over our report afterward. They'll have to investigate. We're moving now." Sylvia smiled. "It feels good."

PART 3

Requite

Chapter 39

Sylvia looked at the packed bags on the den floor. Her neighbor would water her plants and take in her mail. She'd called friends to tell them she'd be out of town for a few days. What had she forgotten?

Sylvia pushed speed dial for Maryanne, silently thanking Erica for putting that in her phone. Calling her was not nearly so frustrating.

"Hello, Maryanne. This is Sylvia. How are you doing?"

"I'm doing better. That last medication the doctor gave me for the urinary tract infection seems to be working. That's a real relief. It took a long time to find the right one. If that boy wasn't so cute, I'd go to another doctor. How's Joe?" Maryanne asked.

"Getting excited about our trip to Virginia. It has been tough on him. He's recovered from being in and out of the hospital, rehab, and the nursing home but still tires. Watching him, I see my future if I don't take care of myself – maybe even if I do."

Maryanne sighed. "I know. There are fewer of us every year."

"Seeing this happen to Joe opened my eyes to my own mortality. I'm determined to not go through that, but I'm not sure what the alternative is.

"This chance to atone for his past has kept Joe going. It's kept me going as well. Reading the accounts and log entries takes me back. It's like I'm alive again. I see myself doing a final check before climbing into that P-51. I feel the rumble, hear the roar of the takeoff as my stomach is left behind. I love it so."

"I know what you mean, Sylvia. We seem to be stumbling through existence today. I wish I were going too, but my doctor forbids it. I'm sure my kids told him to say that." Maryanne sighed.

"I understand. I cancelled my last appointment because mine might say the same thing. Erica is all for it, but my daughter is against it. I'm ignoring her." Sylvia ignored her more and more lately. What was the use of just being alive?

"When are you leaving?"

Sylvia again looked around her den. Pre-trip jitters, she thought. "Our flight is early tomorrow morning. I'm getting a cab. We'll pick up Joe on the way. I don't want to drive in the dark."

"Good luck, Sylvia. Keep your nose above the horizon and your wings straight."

Chapter 40

Sylvia looked at the dashboard in the rented car. Unfamiliar car, unknown roads, doubt that she could do this arose. She took a deep breath. "Okay, Joe, you navigate and I'll drive. Erica printed out a Google Maps route for us that can't miss." The rental car also had a GPS system, but the rental agent's explanation was confusing. She didn't think they could program it.

She followed the signs out of the airport. It was early afternoon, and traffic was light, but the sky was heavy with clouds. The signs to Fredericksburg and Washington D. C. put them on I-95. Traffic got a lot heavier. She was driving just under the speed limit, everybody was passing her, some honking, giving her rude gestures.

"Okay," said Joe, looking at the map. "Stay on the I-95. According to this, it's pretty straightforward." He looked out the window. "It sure is green here. Spring is in full swing."

Sylvia dare not look from the road. The trees seemed too close to the highway, the traffic hemmed her in. It began to sprinkle. She fumbled for the wiper control, longing for the open space and sunny skies of Tucson. "Living in Tucson, we don't see trees like this. How are you feeling?"

"I'm a bit tired from the flight. The last time I came here, it was by train. It took three days. Imagine, seven hours, and we're here."

"Joe, we have time. Why don't you take a little nap?"

"Yeah, I think I will. You won't get lost, will you?"

"I'll be fine." Her hands were already aching from her death grip on the steering wheel. He adjusted the seat and leaned back. Joe worried her. He seemed frail on the plane and in the airport. Silly man. He tried to pick up the bags. That's what porters are for. This past six months, her fondness for him had grown.

She knew the route. Get off at exit 130 A and head east for a mile. Sylvia took a deep breath. She flew planes, she could handle this.

Joe started to snore.

Sylvia fumbled to turn on the headlights. The sky was darker, and the rain had increased, so had traffic. Exit 128 flew by. I need to get in the right-hand lane, she thought. Signaling, she started to change lanes. The blast of the horn of the eighteen-wheeler caused her to swerve back. Where had that semi come from? She slowed to let it pass; the driver behind her began blowing his horn. As exit 129 passed, she found her opening and moved into the exit lane.

Going-home traffic was stop and go. The wipers on high barely kept up with the rain, she strained to look ahead for the Holiday Inn. Like a welcome beacon, she saw it ahead. Easing the car into the entryway, she sat, catching her breath. When had she started holding it?

Unpeeling her fingers from the steering wheel, she nudged Joe. "Wake up. We're here."

His eyelids fluttered. He looked around. "What, already?"

"It wasn't a long drive, it was easy," she lied. "Let's check in and get something to eat. I think we should make an early night of this."

The receptionist gave them adjacent rooms. They were nice. The man helping with the bags thanked them for the tip and left.

"Joe, I'm going to freshen up. I'll meet you downstairs in thirty minutes. Okay?"

He nodded. She watched him slowly move into his room.

At the front desk she asked if there was a Denny's near. Easy, it was close. She helped Joe to the car. "Joe, this traffic is horrible. I'm sure glad we don't see this in Tucson. I'd consider giving up driving." Rush hour was in full swing. Frustration built as they waited for an opening.

"I'm just going to ease out." Horns blared. It took a mere half hour to drive the eight blocks to the yellow Denny's sign. "I'm glad the rain eased up. At least we won't get wet."

Joe was quiet during dinner. That was fine with Sylvia. She was exhausted from the flight and the drive. The thought of the drive back to the motel made her shudder.

By the time they finished dinner, the rain had stopped, and the traffic was lighter.

Joe looked tired as Sylvia helped him up to his room.

At his door, he asked, "What time tomorrow?"

"Let's meet in the lobby at nine-o'clock. We'll stop for breakfast on the way to Lake of the Woods."

"That sounds fine. See you tomorrow." He yawned and closed the door.

Chapter 41

Sylvia, in navy pants and a white blouse, noted Joe's usual tan pants with a checked shirt. She was going to get him some clothes when they got back. Eating at Shonney's was a new experience for her, the display of food available at the buffet amazing. The rest last night and the coffee energized her. Joe looked better too. Traffic was lighter by the time breakfast was over.

"Okay, Joe, according to Erica's map, we travel west on State Route 3 for twenty-five miles to the entrance to Lake of the Woods. That sounds easy enough."

The further they got from Fredericksburg, the lighter the traffic, but at times, the trees closed in, blocking out the sun. Other times, the roadside opened to grassy fields. Signs along the road listed Civil War battle sites she had heard and read about. Chancellorsville flashed by. The ghosts of that war, solemn faced boys in blue and gray, seemed to rise from the fields and hover along the road. Sadness struck her. So great a loss of life in that war.

Her thoughts turned to what was coming. How would Joe handle it? Sylvia glanced at him, a statue staring out the window. "Are you nervous?"

"Yeah, some."

"We'll be fine." She wished she were as sure as she sounded.

The stoplight at Constitution Highway was a landmark. "Lake of the Woods is a mile ahead, Joe." At the next stoplight, she made the left turn. Signs directed her to the visitor's gate. At the barricade, she stopped. They were here. Her stomach fluttered.

The sun had ducked behind a dark cloud. The guard came out of the guardhouse and approached the car. She fumbled with the window button. It hummed down at last.

"May I help you?" the young man asked

Sylvia looked at him. With his uniform, black hair and smooth youthful face, he looked like a Boy Scout. "I'm Sylvia Dunham and this is Joe Clark. We're here to see Allen Rogers."

The guard checked his smart phone. "Is the Senator expecting you? You're not on his visitor list."

"Joe is an old war buddy from Arizona. We're visiting the area and thought we'd stop in and surprise him."

"I'm sorry. The Senator only takes visitors on the list. You can call him and get him to list you, but I can't let you in."

A few raindrops splatted on the windshield. The car behind honked. The guard looked up and waved. Sylvia looked at Joe then back at the guard. "We came all the way from Arizona. Can you call for us?"

The car honked again. He turned back to them. "You'll have to call him."

Sylvia pulled out her cellphone. "Can you give me his number?"

"I can't give his number out. Look, I'm sorry. Why don't you call his son's campaign office and talk to someone there. They can give you his number. Here's the office number." The guard handed her a card. "You can't park here, but go back out to the shopping center across the highway. You can call from there." He pointed behind them.

Sylvia put on her best 'sad little old lady' look. The guard held up his hands then pointed behind her. She looked at the car tight on her bumper, he honked. The guard raised the barricade and gestured to a U-turn lane. "I guess a lot of people don't get in," said Sylvia. For just a second she was tempted make a run for it.

In the parking lot of the grocery store, Joe read the card from the guard. "*Jeff Rogers, Your Senator.* It lists campaign offices in Richmond, Norfolk, Charlottesville, and Fredericksburg."

She dialed. It was busy. "What a disappointment. We drove all this way."

"Sylvia, we can keep trying. Rather than call the Fredericksburg office, let's go by, see if we can get Allen Rogers' phone number."

"You don't want to stay here and try to call again?"

"I think we'll get further face-to-face. It's only a half-hour drive back."

"You're probably right. You navigate."

The sign said 'Jeff Rogers for Senator.' The office was in a small strip mall between a hardware store and a furniture outlet. Posters covered the windows. A young woman greeted them in a soft Southern accent. "Welcome to the Jeff Rogers for Senator campaign headquarters. I'm Shelly. How may I help you?" She tossed her head in a classic cheerleader motion, flicking her blonde hair from her eyes.

Joe spoke first. "I'm Joe Clark and this is Sylvia James. We're visiting from Arizona. I served with the Senator Rogers in World War II, and we'd like to say hi while we're here."

Before she could say anything, a tall man strode through the door. The office grew quiet. He was handsome with light brown hair, perfectly coiffed, and brilliant teeth. He smiled and greeted the people by name, shaking hands and thanking them for their hard work. He stopped in front of them. "Shelly, who do we have here?"

"Mr. Rogers, these people served with your dad during the war. They want to visit with him."

Sylvia stepped forward, holding out her hand. "I'm Sylvia James." She gestured at Joe. "Joe Clark. He served with your dad in Arizona, and we'd like the chance to talk with him – catch up on old times."

Jeff shook her hand and turned toward Joe. "You were stationed at MAAF with Dad?"

"Yes sir, I was," said Joe. "I was a crew chief for him."

"Dad doesn't talk much about his time at MAAF." A high wattage grin crossed his face. He nodded at the idea of surprising his dad. "I'm sure he'll be glad to see you. As it happens, I'm going out to visit Dad in a couple of hours. His health hasn't been good, so let me call first to make sure he'll be up and about. I have a few things to do here. You could follow me out."

"We could disappear for a while and come back," said Sylvia. "Our hotel's not far."

"Joe, Sylvia, I'll give you a call. If you want, we could ride out together. This will be a short visit. Dad's not up to a lot, but I'm sure he'd be glad to see you." He smiled as he entered Joe's cell number on his phone.

Chapter 42

From the passenger seat of Jeff's SUV, Sylvia watched State Route 3 roll by. It was late afternoon, and the sun was alternately hidden behind the trees and blindingly ahead. She was glad someone else was driving. A shiver traveled up her back as she thought of what was ahead. She looked in the back to check on Joe. He stared at the growing shadows as forest sped by. He had been quiet, more than usual.

"Jeff, thank you for offering to drive. Sure it's not an imposition?" asked Sylvia.

"Not at all. When I called this afternoon, he was napping, so this will be a surprise. Mom said she'd get him up for dinner before we get there. I'm really going out to check on Dad, assure him the campaign is going well. I used to believe it was more important to him than to me, but not now. As I've gotten into it, I realize I want to serve my country, and politics is the place I can have the most impact. There are so many things I want to do for people."

Sylvia let that hang. If this was political pap, it would do no good on her. She couldn't vote in Virginia. As they neared Lake of the Woods, her tension rise. She and Joe were heading into the lion's lair to confront him. If she were driving, she'd be tempted to turn around, drive straight to Richmond and catch a plane home.

What thoughts were running through Joe's mind? For almost fifty-six years this had eaten at him. The climax was nigh, and Joe was silent. What was she going to say? She hadn't rehearsed anything, she'd never met the man who was responsible for the deaths of WASPs.

Dusk had deepened into dark. Trees appeared and zoomed past. The stoplight and small shopping center was a welcome island of light. They turned onto the Constitution Highway. Blackness closed in again. Two yellow points of light appeared on the side of the road. Jeff braked hard.

"Deer," he explained as the animal bounded across the road. "You have to watch for them this time of day. Hitting one of those would spoil our trip."

It might be the lesser of two evils shortly, thought Sylvia. A lonely stoplight appeared in the distance. They turned onto Flat Run. A mile later, Jeff turned into another gate, an automatic one.

"This is closer to the house than the front gate," Jeff explained. Through the twists and turns, lights winked at them from the trees. "Here we are," said Jeff, pulling into a well-lit driveway. The expansive yard was well-manicured, with lights framing trees and a fountain. The house at the end of the driveway was huge, easily 6000 square feet. An American flag was spotlighted above the carved double doors.

Joe had stiffened up during the ride. Sylvia helped him from the car. Jeff took his other arm as they mounted the steps. Before Jeff could reach for the door, it opened, framing a petite woman with silver hair in a pageboy cut. She stepped into Jeff's embrace.

"Hi, Mom. How's Dad?" he said as she pulled away.

"You know your father. He can't slow down, totally ignores the doctor's orders. We did move him to the downstairs guestroom until we can get the elevator installed." The woman saw Joe and Sylvia for the first time.

"I'm sorry," said Jeff. "Sylvia James, Joe Clark, this is my mom, Miriam." They shook hands as Miriam showed them in. The entryway floor was marble, the walls paneled in oak. The ceiling soared above them with a brilliant chandelier. Prisms scattered light about the room. The floor changed to maple in the main room. A wide stairway dominated the end of the room.

Joe looked at Sylvia. The magnificent house certainly humbled his apartment at the retirement home. Was this the wages of sin?

"Joe served with Dad in Arizona. They stopped by the campaign office this afternoon, so I invited them to come see Dad. It'll be a surprise."

Joe and Sylvia glanced at each other. It sure would be.

Joe was nervous. Doubts surfaced in his mind. His flight reaction bubbled just below the surface.

Why were they doing this? It wouldn't really change anything. They were about to attack this peaceful scene. Miriam and Jeff seemed to be nice people. He didn't know what to expect with Colonel Rogers.

"Your father's on the porch. He sneaks out there for a smoke after dinner. He thinks I don't know. Can I get you all anything from the bar?" Miriam asked.

"Do you have Southern Comfort?" asked Sylvia.

"Of course we do," answered Miriam. "You want an Old Fashioned? It's my favorite libation." Sylvia nodded. "Joe, what about you?"

"Scotch rocks," said Joe. This seemed so social, like dance music on the Lusitania, unaware of the torpedo speeding their way.

"Jeff, take them into the office. I'll bring your usual Sam Adams." She turned toward the dining room.

Jeff led them through a doorway into an office. Books lined the shelves on the dark wood-paneled walls. A massive desk dominated the area in front of French doors leading to a porch. Lights from across the lake silhouetted a lone figure in a wheelchair.

"Wait here," whispered Jeff.

Joe and Sylvia watched him give the man a hug. Behind them red and green lights drifted through the shimmering reflections as boats moved past on the lake. Jeff stood and wheeled his dad into the office.

The last image of Captain Rogers in Joe's mind was the tall slim man in his spit and polish uniform. The figure in the wheelchair bore no resemblance to that man. He was pale and shriveled, barely filling out his golf shirt. His hair was mere wisps on his age-spotted head. His rummy eyes blinked rapidly. There was no vitality.

"Dad, I brought you a surprise. Do you remember Joe Clark from Marana Army Air Field?"

Rogers had a blank look on his face, obviously not understanding. With the instincts of a politician, he held out his liver-spotted hand. It trembled as Joe took it.

"And, Dad this is Sylvia James. She also served in the war. She was…"

"I was a WASP, a member of the Women's Airforce Service Pilots" said Sylvia. She stepped forward and took Roger's hand. It felt dry, the handshake weak. She looked into his eyes, saw them widen as he began to comprehend who they were.

Miriam wheeled in a cart laden with bottles and glasses. Sylvia and Joe graciously accepted their drinks with thanks. She handed Allen a tumbler of bourbon. "I know you're not supposed to have that, but I thought we'd celebrate. It's your favorite, Maker's Mark. Jeff, here's your beer. How about a toast?" She held up her own Old Fashioned.

Sylvia looked at Rogers. His mouth was slack, his eyes flicked over those around him like a cornered animal. "To the past," she said. "May it never be forgotten." Jeff, Miriam, and Joe raised their glasses. Allen tossed the whole tumbler full down in a gulp and began to cough.

"Lord God Almighty! Allen, I swear. What is wrong with you," Miriam rushed to him and pounded on his back.

Rogers continued to cough, tears in his eyes. Jeff went to help. "Dad, are you all right?"

In a soft voice, Sylvia said, "I think Allen recognizes Joe as a part of his past he thought was buried. Colonel Rogers, you recognize Joe Clark, don't you?"

Miriam and Jeff froze, trying to understand what was happening. Sylvia pulled a file from her large bag. Turning toward Jeff she said, "Here is a collection of incident reports of pilot accidents that happened in World War Two. In a few of them, the pilots, women pilots, were killed or injured, others were minor crashes. Your father was part of a group trying to discredit those pilots."

Jeff stared at her, mouth agape. He looked down at his dad. Rogers' head shook; his trembling hand waved back and forth trying to fend them off. "No," he said weakly.

Sylvia stared hard at Rogers, holding up the folder, continuing. "Some of those incidents weren't accidents. They were sabotage, yet all the investigations reported *pilot error*."

Jeff's gaze flicked from Sylvia to Joe as if they were speaking a foreign language. "What are you saying? What did my father have to do with this?"

Joe spoke. "Captain Rogers was my commanding officer. He ordered me to sabotage a plane I was overhauling. It crashed. The WASP, Mary Anderson, was killed. He then conspired with the investigating team under the command of Jake Williams to report that crash as *pilot error*. It was murder. When I couldn't stay silent any longer I was a threat to him and he shipped me to Alaska for the duration of the war."

A low "No." came from Rogers, his head bowed and his shoulders shaking.

Miriam, her face frozen, stumbled toward her husband.

"Dad…" Jeff started, his hands reaching out to his father. Allen's eyes met Jeff's. "Say this isn't true." He glanced at the file in Sylvia's hand. This had to be a smear campaign. It couldn't be real. He'd get to the bottom of it!

Sylvia watched the shrunken figure in the chair stare at his son. No denial came forth. She and Joe had set Jeff up. He had brought these people into his father's home, and they attacked what was left of his dad. Jeff looked back at his father, his head slowly rising to look at his son.

Everyone waited for a denial.

Rogers glared at Sylvia. His eyes shifted to Joe. "You worthless shit. I kept you from killing yourself. That's what you would have done if you'd stayed at the MAAF. You were weak, couldn't handle what had to be done." His hand rose, crooked finger pointing at Joe. "You were the one who did it," he rasped out.

Jeff's mouth hung open. Resentment radiated from his father. Rogers' hand moved to his heart. Miriam began to slump, stumbling backward. Sylvia caught her, easing her into a chair. "Get your hands off me," Rogers' wife hissed.

The scene was a tableau, frozen in time. Joe felt that a grenade had gone off in the room, all of them hit by shrapnel. The Captain Rogers he knew would have lashed out, counterattacking these accusations, flinging out threats, making accusations, ranting until opposition was destroyed. Now he sat, sapped of strength, a shrunken man.

Sylvia looked at Miriam with concern. She seemed on the edge, trying to marshal her strength to defend him. Not yet able to pull herself together, she was on the verge of collapse. Her gaze moved from her husband to Jeff, pleading for his help.

Joe looked at the floor, stunned by what had happened. He was unsure of what to do next. He had pictured a confrontation with Rogers where he and Sylvia would verbally beat his nemesis down. He hadn't counted in destroying a family.

Sylvia's focus was on Rogers, waiting for a reaction. She glanced at Miriam, a look of compassion crossed her face. The enormity of what had happened starting to dawn on her. She looked at Jeff, then at the door for an escape.

"What are you going to do with that?" Jeff nodded at the file.

She pulled herself together. "It is our intent to get it to the press for release. Those who sacrificed and died for their country deserve that."

Miriam struggled up from the chair. She took a breath, bringing herself erect, pushed her shoulders back, fought to regain her composure. "I think you all should leave," she said, pointing at the door. "Jeffery, take them out of here."

Her words moved them to action. "Dad, will you be okay?" Rogers didn't move. "Mom, will you be all right?"

She nodded her head once. "Just get them out of here. I'll tend to your father."

Chapter 43

Sylvia tried to read Jeff's face by the glow of the dash lights as he drove the SUV to the highway. It was a frozen mask. He broke the silence.

"When are you going to release the files?"

"We haven't set any time," said Sylvia, turning to Joe in the backseat. He appeared to be asleep.

"May I go through them first?" asked Jeff through clenched teeth.

She could tell he was angry with her and Joe. Sylvia felt badly that they had used him. He seemed different from his father, at least from the brief view she'd had.

"Jeff, the confrontation with your dad tonight was something Joe and I had to do. This has been a nightmare to him for more than fifty years." She glanced back at Joe. He seemed frozen, a statue looking out the window, but seeing nothing. "The exposure of these acts is not to hurt your father, but to vindicate those women targeted because they were women trying to do what was right at the time.

"I understand that you have to assure yourself that the facts are true, so sure, this copy of the files is yours. I also understand your anger toward us. We used you badly and hurt your family. You and your mother didn't do these things, but you will suffer. For that, I apologize.

"The evidence we compiled is convincing, but it is Joe's statement that will bring veracity to this sad story." She looked back. Joe still hadn't moved. "As a good attorney, you would probably be able to successfully defeat these charges in a court of law. Public opinion is different."

Jeff's car pulled up to the hotel. "Joe, we're here," Sylvia said.

Joe blinked his eyes several times. He looked around – lost. He tried to open the door – failed. Sylvia opened it, grasped his hand and pulled. Slowly, he emerged from the car.

"I'll call you tomorrow," said Jeff, glancing at the file folder on the seat.

With her arm around Joe, she guided him through the door. His gait was unsteady as he leaned on her. "Joe, let's sit here for a few minutes." She eased him into a lobby chair.

He shrugged off his lethargy. "I guess the look of defeat in Allen eyes was what I wanted and waited for all these years. His mind is still sharp. He realized the consequences of revealing their horrendous plot. It will destroy his legacy. Williams and Marshall are beyond the fallout, but the Army will be forced to investigate. There may be others.

"I feel bad for Jeff and his mother. It was easy to see they never knew anything about this. The release of the report will devastate their lives, too, especially his wife's."

Sylvia nodded. "Allen's wife jumped to defend her husband because he was her husband, not because the report was false. Jeff seems to be a good kid. He'll go through our report like the lawyer he is. He will reach the right conclusion."

"I think so, too." Joe nodded. "This could destroy his run for the Senate."

Sylvia agreed. "His opponent will jump on this."

"I need to think this over," said Joe in a soft voice. "Who will this revenge fall on? It was revenge on my part, for the death of Mary and Dawn, for fifty years of agony. But I didn't consider who else would be hurt. Airing the sabotage and murder is the right thing to do, but to what end? I feel… empty now. The driving force that kept me going is gone, and I'm… I'm tired. I need to go to my room."

"I'll take you up," said Sylvia, assisting him from the chair.

Chapter 44

Miriam looked at the unmoving shape of Allen sitting in his wheelchair. How dare those people attack her husband!

"Allen, do you want me to take you to your room, help you get ready for bed?" asked Miriam. She was concerned about him. He looked so vulnerable, something she'd never seen in him before.

"I'm going to stay here for a while. It's a nice evening," came his weak reply.

She couldn't just stand there. She needed time to regroup. The consequences of that fallacious report would be horrible. Surely, Jeff would find a way to prevent the release.

"Don't forget to take your heart pill. They're on your desk," directed Miriam. "Allen, I'm sorry those people were here. They upset you, they upset all of us. What they talked about, what happened decades ago, it's old news. I don't believe a word of it. You shouldn't worry. I'm going up to read. Ring me when you're ready for bed. Don't be too late." She closed the office door behind her.

Allen Rogers looked through the windows at the dark lake. The boats had gone home for the night, and only a few reflections shimmered from lights in the houses across the lake. The haunting notes of Pink Floyd's *Dark Side of the Moon* from somebody's stereo drifted on the wind.

He picked up the bottle of pills and a bottle of water and wheeled himself onto the porch. The demons of his past were on his doorstep. They had caught up with him, but now he wouldn't be the only casualty.

He no longer had the contacts to hush this up, nor the strength to fight. A lonely future awaited him, Miriam too. This would sink Jeff. The look on Jeff's face stabbed him in his already weakened heart. He thought it had stopped again when they locked eyes. What really drove the stake in was the look of disgust in Jeff's eyes.

Allen fumbled with the pill bottle, taking one out and swallowing it. What a hell of a year. The doctors said he might recover most of his faculties, but deep down he knew better. The thoughts of a future with people whispering behind his back, knowing looks on their faces, watching Miriam try to keep her head up through it all, of letting his son down, drove him to despair. He looked at the bottle, took another pill out. Pinching it between thumb and finger, he held it up.

Across the lake, the lights went out. Darkness stared at him.

The phone awakened Jeff. With bleary eyes, he stared down at the scattered pages of the file in front of him. The phone rang again. What time was it? Who would be calling at this hour? He mumbled "Hello."

"Jeff, something's happened with your father." Miriam sobbed and caught her breath. "The ambulance is here now." Her voice was ragged, her breath coming in gasps.

"I'll be right out," he said, coming instantly awake.

The house was ablaze with light when he pulled up, the door opened to the screech of his tires. His mom held onto the doorframe for support. She fell into his arms as he reached her. He helped her inside to the couch as she sobbed into his chest.

"Mom, what happened?"

Gasping for breath, she said, "He wanted to stay in the office for a while, so I went up to bed. I needed to think before tucking him in. I must have fallen asleep. When I went down, he was in his chair on the porch." She opened her fist revealing the empty pill bottle. "I found this and picked it up. He wasn't breathing. If only I hadn't fallen asleep," she moaned. "I called 911. The EMTs arrived quickly, but it was too late. I never should have left him!" she cried.

"Mom, it's not your fault." Bitterness rose in Jeff toward Sylvia and Joe, but also toward his father for doing this to his mother.

"I know! It's those people who accused him of those vile things!" she spat.

Jeff said nothing. He realized it wasn't their doing either. There would never be a time to explain that to his mother. He held her. Would this night ever end?

Chapter 45

Sylvia's sleep had been fitful, filled with dreams and worries. She had been up for more than an hour when the phone rang. It must be Joe. Good, she was hungry.

"Sylvia, this is Jeff. I'm outside your hotel. I need to talk to you. Would you like breakfast?"

Jeff! She hadn't expected to hear from him so soon. Cautiously she asked, "Now? I haven't heard from Joe yet this morning. He was pretty tired last night."

"It's okay. We can talk; you can fill him in later. Just come to the lobby when you're ready."

There was a strained tone to his voice. A doubt surfaced in her mind. It would be fine, she assured herself. Within ten minutes, Sylvia hurried downstairs. Jeff's appearance startled her. His clothes, the same ones he wore last night, were wrinkled as if he'd slept in them. His face was lined and gray, his eyes dark and puffy, hair disheveled.

"I've just had the worst night of my life. Let's go sit in the coffee shop."

With steaming cups of coffee in front of them, Jeff said, "Your revelation about my dad shocked me. I also shocked myself because I had no trouble believing it. I read the file. It's a compelling story." He held up a hand as Sylvia started to speak. "That's only the start. Mom called me hours later. My dad died last night." Jeff wiped tears from his cheeks. He bowed his head.

Sylvia's mouth dropped. "I'm so sorry. Was it his heart?"

"It wasn't an accident," said Jeff. He looked at her, his face a reflection of misery.

Sylvia gasped. There was no doubt it was the result of their confrontation. "How's your mother?" Guilt flooded in.

"My wife is with Mom now. She's taking it hard. She blames you and Joe for upsetting him."

"Jeff, we didn't intend for this to happen."

"This was my father's doing." Jeff looked into her eyes. "It's something he started decades ago. It finally caught up to him. When I looked into his eyes last night, there was no remorse. He was sorry he was found out. I believe he was sorry that this story would harm Mom and my run for Senate. He did not regret what he did." Jeff's eyes stared at the ceiling for a minute. He sighed. "That was my father. I saw it a long time ago."

Sylvia mulled over Jeff's statement. He <u>was</u> different from his father. Part of her began to regret the fallout of their confrontation. Jeff was staring at his coffee cup, idly turning it.

"Jeff, will this derail your campaign?"

He looked up at her question. A sad smile crossed his face. "I'm going to withdraw tomorrow."

"But, Jeff…"

He waved her objection away. "No, I couldn't win, and I'd be wasting a lot of money."

"I'm sorry, Jeff. Let me talk the release date over with Joe."

"Sure, whatever you want. Call me this afternoon. Here's your file."

"The file is yours, keep it."

Jeff rose. "I need to be with Mom."

Alone at the table, Sylvia stared into her coffee cup, as if answers hid there.

Chapter 46

Deep in thought, Sylvia walked back to her room. Still no Joe. She'd expected he would wander into the coffee shop while she ate. But he didn't. Outside his room, she raised her hand to knock. Peeking under the door was the corner of an envelop. Pulling it out, she saw it was addressed to her. With apprehension, she opened it.

Dear Sylvia,

Last night was the end of a long ordeal for me. I felt no satisfaction when Rogers realized his life was destroyed, only pity. The look that passed between Jeff and him tore his soul out. Everything he'd built in his life crashed down in that moment. His wife jumped to his defense, not because she didn't believe it, but because she is his wife and had to defend him. He had her loyalty. I admired her for that.

Our confrontation destroyed Rogers, but it also will destroy his wife and his son's aspirations. I feel guilty about that. They are innocents in this.

I hadn't foreseen the all of the consequences of what we did. Bad as Rogers is, he did achieve one grand thing in this life., that is Jeff. The more I watched him, the more I realized he is the opposite of his father, exactly the type of person I want to run this country. If we release this report that chance will never happen. I thought it would be over after last night, but it isn't, and I don't have the drive to keep going.

I am so weary. A great weight was lifted from my shoulders when I at last confronted my tormentor. Mary and

Dawn have been avenged. Revenge was not so sweet for me, but it was something I had to do. I owed them that. Now at last I can sleep. I think my ticker is about to tick its last.

Goodbye,

Forever yours, Joe

Sylvia's hand trembled as she raised it to knock. She paused. Joe wasn't in there. She turned slowly and walked to her room, her cheeks streaked and wet. This wasn't what she had planned. What had she envisioned?

She sat at her desk, tears falling on Joe's letter, smearing the ink. The hard edge to her had wanted to strike out, hurt those responsible for murdering her sisters. What she really wanted was to destroy the bias, small mindedness, and prejudice that led to those actions. She and her sisters had struck a mighty blow against them by just becoming WASP. It was a blow that resounded today more strongly than ever before.

The WASP had sacrificed for more than their country at war. They had given for an ideal. She remembered General Hap Arnold's words when the WASP were disbanded:

"When we needed you, you came through and have served most commendably under very difficult circumstances, but now the war situation has changed and the time has come when your volunteer services are no longer needed. The situation is that if

you continue in service, you will be replacing instead of releasing our young men. I know the WASP wouldn't want that. I want you to know that I appreciate your war service and the AAF will miss you... "

They had put their lives on hold and at risk so the young men could go and fight evil in the world. Today another fight was taking place – not in the air over foreign countries, but in the halls of Congress.

Chapter 47

Sylvia poured her iced tea and sat in the easy chair. Since her return from Virginia, the fire of the hunt had subsided giving way to the fog of age. It had been difficult getting Joe's body back to Tucson. She was able to take possession, but the interstate transport was hard. Jeff helped her with the paperwork and permits. Thank God for him.

With help from the VA, she'd made the arrangements for Joe's cremation. There was nobody to attend a service, so she and Erica drove to the Pinal Airpark, the old MAAF. They scattered half of his ashes in the desert. She watched aircraft overhead as they came and went, tears drying on her cheeks.

What a change that war created. The whole country participated, not just soldiers. It built a level of loyalty not seen since. Centuries of traditional roles were transformed. The available workforce, the available brainpower, was doubled. This basic change in society took place in only a few decades.

She sadly thought of those countries saddled with old-style conventions trying to compete in the world. It was like a boxer trying to fight with one hand tied behind his back. And the WASP, the Rosie the Riveters, the factory workers initiated a world-changing society. How far they had come!

Ah Joe, she thought, you brought purpose back into my life. While I was with you, we had force and direction. In the end, you were right. There was no one left to take the blame, only innocents to hurt. Our world isn't the same. We have learned to be better. Thank you for showing me honor and compassion. For a while, you brought me new life. Is it time to grow old? Perhaps.

The drive back with Erica was quiet. Entering her house, Erica turned on the television while Sylvia placed Joe's urn on the shelf beside Harold's. She hung her wings over the urn. You deserve this, Joe, she thought. You were one of us.

"Grandma, come look at this," called Erica.

A scene of Jeff Rogers was on the screen. Sylvia perked up.

"In a hotly contested race for senator in Virginia, Jeff Rogers has been proclaimed the winner. He made the following statement in his acceptance speech."

The camera showed Jeff at the podium in front of his cheering supporters. He held up his hands to quiet the crowd.

"First, I want to thank all of you for your support and faith in me. I will work tirelessly to do what's right for Virginia and for people. One of my first tasks upon assuming office is something long overdue. During the final days of the campaign, I learned a lesson from some World War II heroes who gave their time and in some cases their lives for this country. That group is the Women Airforce Service Pilots. They took over the dangerous job of flying military aircraft within the United States so our fighting men could go overseas. They received little recognition. I will push for them to be awarded the Congressional Gold Medal as a token of thanks for their service."

He held up Sylvia's file.

"There were instances of crimes committed against them because they were women doing what some thought were men's jobs. That prejudice, those crimes cannot remain hidden, for we must learn what not to do ever again. Press copies of this report will be released this afternoon, and I'm turning it over to the Department of the Army for investigation."

I look forward to being your senator, representing you in making this country better. Thank you.

The camera cut back to the reporter.

"That was a little different from most acceptance speeches. We look forward to more information."

Sylvia wiped tears from her eyes. She looked at the two urns on her bookshelf.

"Wow, Grandma. The son of the man you went to confront is going to pursue this!"

"Erica, there are honorable people in this world. Joe was one. It looks like Jeff is too."

She smiled. "One thing this country needs is to be allowed to have heroes again. Real people, not imaginary caped crusaders. Heroes are not defined by how they look, but what they do. Mostly, they are ordinary people with honor who stand up for what is right." Now where were her glasses?

Author's Note

Although much of the information in this novel is factual, the story of Joe Clark is fiction. Names have been made up or changed. Events have sprung from my imagination. I don't think any of the WASP believe there was an organized conspiracy or sabotage against them. I'm not so trusting, but then I wasn't of their generation, nor was I there.

The incident in the retirement home did happen to my mom. A man did approach her as she was picking up her uniform and claim that a fatal crash of a WASP occurred in Marana. He did not say it was sabotage, only that they had failed to remove those service plugs from the engine. Mom and I went home and looked up the incident. It was real, though the pilot was not killed. It was listed as *Pilot Error*. That started my thinking that it was time for a story.

Numerous documentaries and accounts have been written about the WASP. There have been documentary movies and news articles done on them extolling their bravery in stepping into the man's world of flying for the military. Mom and I attended a reunion in Sweetwater where a B-1 bomber flew in with an all female crew. Without the WASP, that would not have happened.

I attended other reunions, and like a kid around the campfire, listened to the stories these women told, my eyes aglow. A few of the stories were about sabotage, but far more were of the astonishment members of the military displayed when these brave little gals flew even the most powerful war machines on the planet. To them it was a great adventure.

Today there are far too few of them left, and not nearly enough accounts of their adventures. This was a period in our history when prejudice and bias were common, and breaking out of that mold could be dangerous. Lorraine Rogers did have her rudder cables cut and barely escaped with her life. Sabotage was not indicated in the incident report.

Texas Women's University is the repository for much of their history. I urge you to look further into what they hold. It took people like Barry Goldwater and Kay Bailey Hutcheson to get the WASP the acknowledgement they deserved for being the first.

My heart jumped into my throat when I saw my mom's uniform hanging in a museum near her hometown. It was sent there from the Pima Air and Space Museum after they changed their displays.

My mom did go to California after her WASP service to work on the engine of the first jet airplane project in the U.S. It was there she met my dad. (Yeah, the rest is history)

It is true that the women had to take up collections to get the bodies of those killed back to their loved ones at home. It is true that when the WASP were disbanded they were thanked and told to go away – no train or bus fare. But not one of them wouldn't do it all again.

Bless you Mom. I know you're in that P-51 with the throttle at the firewall climbing into the clouds.

For me, writing is not a solo activity. It requires the help, support, and assistance of many people. Without my editors, this would not have happened, certainly not in the polished form it is now. It was Melinda Rucker Haynes, Carol Bondurant, Mary Corey, and Chaitali Banerjee of the *Tall Grass Editing CoOp* who held my feet to the fire to make this better, showing me little mercy. Alexis Powers prodded me to finish this book and helped edit it to get to the final version. Her Oro Valley Writers Motivational Workshop has helped many authors to publish, and opened the community of writers to me. What fun these people are! Thanks to you all.

www.ingramcontent.com/pod-product-compliance
Lightning Source LLC
Chambersburg PA
CBHW030614170726
48283CB00002B/605